Marlee melted against Matteo and he could feel her cheek on his back.

"Let's pretend," she suggested gleefully. "You're an Italian beach bum, and I'm an outlaw pretending to be a librarian."

He was going to say "Let's not," but her face had a light in it—playful, invigorated, alive—that would take a man much stronger than him to put out.

"I've never been on a motorbike before," she called.

"Calling it a motorbike is a stretch," he called back to her. "It's a scooter."

"Whatever it is, it's awesome. Go faster!"

He thought they were probably at about maximum speed already—in every single way—but if he could squeeze a little more power out of the machine, did that mean she would cling harder? He couldn't help himself. He had to find out.

And just like that, it was awesome: the wind, the sun, the charms of the island, a beautiful woman clinging to him. Matteo did something he rarely did.

He surrendered to the day.

He was pretty sure he was lost in more ways than one.

Dear Reader,

My friends Bill and Rose are to gardens what I hope I am to writing. They transform empty—or even ugly—spaces into places of pure magic.

Thanks to them, my garden (I used to call it a yard!) has become the most inspiring of places. Uniquely beautiful, some of its spaces vibrate with ever-changing color and energy and light, and others—deeply shaded—offer room for tranquility and introspection.

This story really flowed from the solitude of early morning in the sanctuary that Bill and Rose created for me.

In that garden, I am reminded of how interconnected all our gifts are, and I am deeply grateful for that awareness.

My wish is that my gift brings you, the reader, moments of pure wonder, just like those I have received from Bill and Rose.

With best wishes,

Cara Colter

Bahamas Escape with the Best Man

—

Cara Colter

HARLEQUIN
Romance

HARLEQUIN®

Romance™

Recycling programs
for this product may
not exist in your area.

ISBN-13: 978-1-335-40716-0

Bahamas Escape with the Best Man

Copyright © 2022 by Cara Colter

For questions and comments about the quality of this book,
please contact us at CustomerService@Harlequin.com.

Harlequin Enterprises ULC
22 Adelaide St. West, 41st Floor
Toronto, Ontario M5H 4E3, Canada
www.Harlequin.com

Printed in U.S.A.

Cara Colter shares her life in beautiful British Columbia, Canada, with her husband, nine horses and one small Pomeranian with a large attitude. She loves to hear from readers, and you can learn more about her and contact her through Facebook.

Books by Cara Colter

Harlequin Romance

A Fairytale Summer!

Cinderella's New York Fling

Cinderellas in the Palace

His Convenient Royal Bride
One Night with Her Brooding Bodyguard

A Crown by Christmas

Cinderella's Prince Under the Mistletoe

Matchmaker and the Manhattan Millionaire
His Cinderella Next Door
The Wedding Planner's Christmas Wish
Snowbound with the Prince

Visit the Author Profile page
at Harlequin.com for more titles.

To Bill and Rose Pastorek, with deepest gratitude
for how generously they have shared their gifts
with me.

**Praise for
Cara Colter**

"Ms. Colter's writing style is one you will want
to continue to read. Her descriptions place you
there.... This story does have a HEA but leaves you
wanting more."

—*Harlequin Junkie* on *His Convenient Royal Bride*

CHAPTER ONE

"Sir, we'll be landing in a few minutes."

Matteo Keller opened his eyes. He wasn't sure if he'd been sleeping, or just drifting.

Either was unusual. Usually, he found the time on board his company's private jet to be perfect for catching up on work, uninterrupted.

He had a well-honed jet lag strategy where he used the flight time to start resetting his inner clock from the time in Zurich to the time zone he would be arriving in.

Definitely sleeping, he thought, bemused, as he looked at the business papers that had slid from his tabletop desk and now lay around him. So much for his jet lag strategy. The sun was setting out there, and now he was wide-awake.

Right on top of the scattered papers was a brochure, shiny and colorful. Matteo picked it up. It described his destination, one of the two thousand four hundred cays and seven hundred islands that formed the Bahamas.

Coconut Cay, the safest place on earth.

Glancing at the pictures of the boutique hotel, the white sands and the turquoise waters of the island, Matteo was not sure why safety had been picked as the main selling feature of the tropical paradise. If he was in charge of marketing...

You're not, he told himself firmly.

And maybe there *was* something to be said for the brochure's claim that doors could be left unlocked and your watch would be safe on the bedside table.

Well, maybe not *his* watch.

According to the brochure, the tiny island, which had several resorts and one village, had a zero crime rate, and each guest was carefully vetted.

He did vaguely remember his assistant asking him questions that had seemed, at the time, both mildly intrusive and slightly irritating.

Welcome to Sullivan's Island, he thought, calling it after a very old and very corny American sitcom about an unlikely group of people shipwrecked.

The island, as the jet descended, seemed idyllic, drowsy and gilded in gold. No doubt safe.

And yet he, of all people, knew that danger lurked in life itself. No matter how hard you tried, there would always be events out of your control, waiting to blow your world to smithereens.

Matteo was taken aback at himself.

That was what he got for dozing, instead of working, for not adhering to his rigid schedule to avert jet lag.

Those were unwanted thoughts, slipping outside of his customary discipline, his ability not to think of the world he had once had or lament how quickly it had slipped away.

He sincerely hoped *the safest place on earth* was not going to make a run at his carefully constructed barriers.

The plane touched down.

"It won't," Matteo told himself tersely, rising from his seat, "because I won't let it."

And yet here it was, nighttime, and he was wide-awake. And for some reason, when he disembarked the plane, he left the scattered business papers—his balm—behind.

Marlee Copeland decided she absolutely hated destination weddings. This was her third one in the past two years.

Admittedly, Coconut Cay was the most beautiful of the three. The small tropical island was extraordinary: gorgeous beaches, calm waters, rainbow-hued flowers the size of basketballs, mangoes, coconuts and banana clusters hanging in trees.

The resort was like something out of a dream.

The color palette of the structures, inside and out, was creamy whites and soothing beiges, everything subdued and extraordinarily tasteful, in sharp and deliberate contrast to the vibrant backdrop of the island.

"So, what's to hate?" Marlee asked herself, the warm air—so different than the November dreariness she had left behind in Seattle—caressing her.

She was standing in darkness that felt somehow silky on her skin, on the pathway outside the private cabana she had wisely paid extra for instead of sharing accommodations with the other bridesmaids.

Night had fallen with the suddenness of a dark blanket being dropped over the sky, and she watched the stars wink out, one by one, and then a rising moon paint the caps of the gentle waves nearby in silver. She listened to them lap on shore. In the distance, she could hear laughter and voices at the pool.

The bridal side of the wedding party. Fiona, bride-to-be, had suggested they arrive a few days early, though not to unwind, as one might think after all the stress of planning a wedding three thousand miles from home.

No, the early arrival was to get rid of the "pasty" look. For the photos. Which had to be perfect, naturally. Marlee was fairly certain

Fiona had cast her a glance when she made the "pasty look" comment.

Or maybe the bride's choice of a dress for her had just made her overly sensitive. Marlee sighed. She knew she should join them, of course. But she didn't want to. The fact she hated it all was just going to be too evident, no matter how hard she tried to hide it.

"What's to hate?" she asked herself again. A night bird chattered as palm fronds swayed in a faint breeze, the air faintly perfumed.

It was all so *romantic*.

And *perfect*.

And *that* was what Marlee hated. All the weddings she had been to lately—and there had been many as her friends were at that age where they were ready for the "next stage" in life—were like this. Romantic and perfect.

Admittedly, her cynicism had set in after her own wedding had fallen through, cancellation notices sent and her elaborate wedding gown boxed up and sent to the thrift store. Before that, at every wedding she'd attended, she had made notes, gleaned ideas and admired dresses.

This was the first wedding since her own matrimonial debacle. Now she felt weddings—including the one she hadn't had—were pure theater, where everyone played their part, especially the beautiful, joyous bride and the handsome, devoted groom, with eyes only for each other. It was pageantry, blind to the statistics that said it probably wasn't going to work out in quite the way the glowing bride and the besotted groom hoped.

Despite how justifiable Marlee's skepticism around weddings might have been, she knew in her heart that she was kidding herself. She still yearned for all that romance to be true.

"You're jealous," Marlee decided.

Was she? Of course! She was supposed to have had all this. Planning *her* day had consumed the better part of her life for over a year.

No destination wedding for her, because of her huge extended family, but instead a gorgeous old church and a posh hotel…and then, the exit by her fiancé, Arthur, just six months ago, embarrassingly close to their spring wedding date.

Even with the help of sympathetic—make that pitying—family members and friends, canceling everything and letting people know there would be no wedding had been nearly as much work as putting it all together.

Add to that the humiliation…

Jilted at the altar.

"I'm *not* jealous," Marlee ordered herself. She was just tired. There was only a three-hour time difference between this tiny island and her home, but the crazy fifteen-hour travel schedule

from Seattle to Florida, onward to Nassau, and
then finally to Coconut Cay, had left Marlee exhausted and discombobulated. Really, she didn't
know if it was time to get up or time to go to
bed. Should she have supper now or breakfast?

The other destination weddings she had attended had not required quite so much effort to
get there.

Now everything felt like too much. They had
barely been whisked to the resort from the tiny
airport when Fiona had rounded them all up and
herded them into her luxurious suite for the big
reveal: the bridesmaid's dresses.

They were Fiona's "surprise" to her girlfriends
who were standing up with her, a gift intended to
in some way assuage the huge financial and time
commitment involved in saying yes to being a
part of a destination wedding. She had collected
all their measurements and refused to reveal any
details of the custom-made dresses. Until now.

*Until they were trapped here and couldn't say
no*, Marlee thought, perhaps unkindly.

There were three bridesmaids and the dresses
were all the same color—hideous. Fiona called
it sea foam, but Marlee thought it looked like
the Spanish moss that hung in creepy fingers
from cypress trees in the Southern parts of the
United States.

Though the same color, each dress purported

to reflect the personality of the person it had been bestowed upon.

So Kathy's had narrow straps and a form-hugging bodice. The short, full skirt flirted around her long legs and accentuated a subtle but undeniable sexiness. Kathy looked like she had been at the tanning booth for at least a month. Nothing pasty about her!

Brenda's dress was a sleek, strapless sheath that, even while hugging her curves, hinted at a woman in control, and indeed, Brenda was CEO of a huge cosmetics company. That company had made their name—and a considerable fortune—on a tanning product called Beach-in-a-Bottle, so Brenda looked sun-kissed and glowing at all times.

And then there was Marlee's. It was, sadly, the dress of the high-school-girl-trying-too-hard variety. In fact, the dress sang *future librarian gets invited to a prom.* Never mind that she *was* a librarian—and had the pasty complexion to prove it! The dress was high-collared and short-sleeved, and abounded with puff and ruffles.

And, as if the dress in and of itself was not like something out of a nightmare, Fiona had gushingly proclaimed, "It's *so* you, Marlee."

And the others had agreed!

After the great reveal, Fiona had ordered them all to their own rooms to change out of the precious garments, and then suggested meeting at the pool for drinks and hors d'oeuvres.

But Marlee was still here outside her cabana—not as luxurious as Fiona's suite, but still beachy and charming—not changed, and despite being starving, was not going to the pool. The highly orchestrated schedule was already giving her a headache.

Not to mention a niggling but growing sense of rebellion.

Her cabana had come with a complimentary travel-size bottle of rum and a cigar. Apparently, the island was famous for both.

Marlee had never smoked a cigar. Ever. And she had certainly never drunk rum straight, but no mix had been provided.

In defiance of how that horrible dress said she was perceived—by those who supposedly knew her best—she cracked the rum open and held the cigar between her fingertips, liking the way that felt—bold and glamourous in an old movie kind of way. If her friends were to see her now, they would get the message.

You don't know me at all.

She took a tentative sip of the rum. Her eyes watered. She choked. On her empty stomach, it was like swallowing fire.

Still, something warm and bold and lovely unfolded in her. She took another tentative sip of the rum and even looked at the cigar, considering whether she should light it.

That was when she became aware she was no longer alone.

The curving pathway that wound around the cabanas on its way to the beach was only faintly lit, solar lights twinkling in the deep, flower-threaded foliage on either side of it, but she could see a man was coming toward her.

In Seattle, alone outside on a dark night, she probably would have ducked back inside. But there was a light on in the cabana next door to hers, and through its open doors she could hear the faint sounds of people talking. Plus, she remembered the brochure's promise that this was the safest place on earth.

The hotel had even sent a pre-arrival questionnaire to make sure they were not inviting criminals or miscreants into their island paradise.

So, chances of the man coming down the walkway being an ax murderer were largely reduced.

Besides which, she felt holding the cigar and sipping rum straight from the bottle asked her to be a different person, not quite so timid, not quite so willing to play it safe.

So, instead of moving away, Marlee watched the man approach. He was one of *those* men. You could tell by the way he moved. Not quite a swagger, but something smooth, confident and totally self-assured was in every step of that long stride.

The white towel draped around his neck was practically glowing against the darkness of the night.

He didn't have a shirt on, and as he got closer, the magnificence of him was fully revealed to her.

He was like a poster boy for *perfect*. Wide shoulders, a broad chest, faint lines of ribs under taut skin, a flat, hard belly that dipped into boldly colored swim shorts, the bareness of his legs showing off how long and sculpted with muscle they were. He was barefoot.

Really, Marley told herself sternly, there was nothing sexy about that. Barefoot went with the beach. He was obviously on his way for a swim.

In the ocean. Not the pool. In the darkness. By himself.

Okay. There was something a little sexy about that. Or maybe a lot.

Or maybe not. He'd probably heard all that feminine giggling at the pool and made a fast detour toward the ocean.

Some instinct stopped him in his tracks then and he squinted up the walkway in her direction. The moon painted silver tips in his dark hair and gilded his face, which was as perfect as the rest of him.

He seemed unfairly handsome, exactly the kind of man who never paid any kind of attention to a woman like her.

Marlee resisted, again, the impulse to slide back toward her open, French-paned door. Wasn't it exactly that shrinking librarian attitude that had earned her this dress?

CHAPTER TWO

AT THAT EXACT MOMENT, the man spotted her in the shadows. He hesitated, then moved forward cautiously, as if he knew a shrinking librarian when he saw one.

"I'm sorry," he said. "I didn't mean to startle you."

Since Marlee was trying very hard not to look startled, his apology was annoying. Still, if she was going to be startled, eyes like his would do it. In the faint illumination of the pathway lights and the moon, they seemed as turquoise as the sea had been before darkness fell.

"According to the resort map, I think this is the only way to the beach."

Now he was practically apologizing for using a public path. Exactly how buttoned-up did she look? Well, there was the dress, which she had not taken off, despite Fiona's orders. Perhaps she thought a few swigs of rum could improve it.

She was counting on the the cigar and the rum bottle, now to be contradicting the message of the dress!

His voice was rich and deep and reassuring

in some way. She heard a faint and intriguing accent. The old Marlee—the one she had been just minutes ago, before being presented with this dress—would have just nodded, smiled politely and watched him move away, resigned to being dismissed.

"It seems like an odd time to indulge in a swim," she said, not quite flirting, but not retiring, either. *Engaging* him. She took a defiant swig of the rum.

Both the rum and engaging him felt deliciously dangerous in how terribly out of character they were for her.

He tilted his head toward her, faint surprise crinkling around his astounding eyes, making her notice they were fringed in lusciously abundant lashes.

"I've been working all day," he said. "There were some unexpected challenges. I need to clear my mind."

So he worked here. At Coconut Cay. She wondered what he did. Management of some sort, no doubt. There was something in the way he carried himself that suggested he dealt with people, and he was good at it. She wondered if those unexpected challenges he'd dealt with today had anything to do with Fiona's arrival, and was practically certain that they did.

"Well, I'm sure a midnight swim is good for

that," Marlee said, though she wasn't sure at all. What did she know about midnight swims? She felt a sudden, sharp and somewhat shocking yearning for worlds unexplored.

Now that he was stopped, he was apparently quite happy to *engage*. His eyes trailed to the unlit cigar in her right hand. A smile twitched, drawing her attention to white, straight teeth, the fullness of his bottom lip.

Something happened to the air. It went from soft, and faintly perfumed, to charged, a before-the-storm intensity humming through it.

Marlee found herself entranced by him, and either emboldened by the rum—or by the persona she had indulged by holding the cigar as if she knew what to do with it—she took a long, leisurely look at him. It felt like a drink of cold water on a hot day.

More perfection.

His hair was a little long, tucked behind his ears, the feathered tips riding his shoulders. It was very straight, dark and milk chocolate strands sewn together. He had high cheekbones, a straight nose and full, sensual lips.

There was a scent coming off him, as if his golden-toned skin had absorbed sunshine all day and was now emitting that tantalizing smell.

She was suddenly way too aware that she likely smelled of a day's travel overlaid with rum, but it didn't stop her from wondering if his skin would feel as warm as it smelled. Her fingertips had this funny little itch in them.

To touch him. A complete stranger. Ridiculous! She was not that kind of girl.

Though, for the first time in her life, Marlee was aware of maybe wanting to be.

She noted again that his eyes were—impossibly—as turquoise as the waters of the bay.

"Speaking of odd indulgences..." he said. "Cigars and rum at midnight?"

Marlee noticed that thread of humor that totally confident men always had in their tone in his voice.

"Actually, I don't think it is midnight," she said.

The stranger did not seem the least insulted by Marlee's tone, which may have been faintly querulous in the face of his sheer attraction, his easy confidence, and a whole different world his mere presence was letting her know she missed.

He lifted a shoulder. "You suggested it first. *Midnight* swim?" he reminded her.

"It's just a turn of phrase."

"Ah," he said, utterly composed. Of course, he no doubt spent his days dealing with cranky, demanding tourists, and soothing them with his deep, accented voice and his lovely eyes. In fact, his smile deepened. "It's midnight somewhere."

He'd know that, too, dealing as he did, with guests from all over the world.

He had a dimple, just on one side.

"Are you going to smoke that?" he asked, nodding to the cigar in her hand.

Apparently she *was* diverting attention from the sheer ugliness of the dress as he appeared not to have noticed it yet.

"I'm thinking of it," she lied, as if she was sophisticated and mysterious and smoked cigars all the time.

Unfortunately, that made her feel as if she had to prove something. She put it to her nose and sniffed it, something she was fairly sure an expert would do before lighting it.

He lifted a wicked slash of a dark eyebrow at her. "First time?"

So much for sophisticated and mysterious. He wasn't fooled. She wasn't sure how he managed to make those two words—first time?—sound quite so naughty.

She could pretend it wasn't her first time, but there seemed no point.

"What gave me away?"

"You're holding it as if you thought you had picked up a friendly neighborhood cat, but you've just realized it was a skunk, instead."

Marlee felt an unusual tickle. It wasn't the

cigar. It was a giggle, and it shocked her, because she was not a giggler.

At all.

Could she chock that up to two or three mouthfuls of rum? Doubtful, no matter how strong the island rum was. It was him, teasing something girlish to the surface in her. So he was charming as well as handsome. He should come with a flashing neon sign.

Danger.

Again, though, if he dealt with people all day every day, this would be his skill set. Charming. Setting people at ease.

"I might smoke it," she said.

"Ah. And what would be the occasion for your first cigar?"

Was he just being conversational, or did he find her interesting? The possibility nearly tied knots in her tongue.

"People should try new things."

He cocked his head at her. "Forgive me for being presumptuous, but you don't look like the kind of woman who would voluntarily try anything that comes with a health warning on it."

Well, that either meant she looked healthy. Or like a nerd.

"It's the dress," she admitted reluctantly.

Why had she said that? First cigars were about celebrations: babies, job promotions… Instead, she had directed his attention to the full horror of her attire. The dress practically screamed wedding, and Marlee didn't actually want him to know she was a member of the demanding wedding party that was driving him into the sea in the darkness in hopes of clearing his head.

He regarded her attire solemnly and at length. She experienced the full, mesmerizing enchantment of the amazing color of his eyes and their framing in a decadent abundance of sooty lash.

She refused to squirm under a gaze that might be called stripping.

"That dress inspired the loss of cigar virginity?" he finally asked.

The word *virginity* coming from his mouth felt as if he had said something naughty and personal, especially since his thorough inspection had left her feeling as if something was tingling along her skin.

He didn't seem to recognize it as a bridesmaid's dress.

"It's vugly," she said.

He tilted his head. "I'm sorry. English is my second language. I'm rarely caught out, but I don't know that word."

"My own creation: vugly. A combination of very and ugly."

Her creativity was rewarded with a smile tickling the luscious sensuality of those lips.

"Vugly," he said, and gave a pleased chortle. "I'll have to file that one away for future use."

Yes, Marlee thought, it might be a useful addition to his vocabulary. He could use it to describe a bride having a temper tantrum over some tiny detail not quite right.

"Besides the fact it's vugly," Marlee went on, "it's frilly and fussy and it scratches."

"Where?" he asked, softly.

He managed to make that sound naughty, too, as if he could aid her in some way.

"Everywhere!"

"Ah," he said. He took a step back from her and studied the dress even more carefully. Those dark slashes of brows lowered in a thoughtful frown.

"It doesn't seem *you*, somehow," he decided.

At his proclamation, Marlee was sure she felt the ground shift under her feet, like rock crumbling in warning right before a cliff.

A complete stranger had *seen* her, when her own girlfriends had not. It made him even more compelling than he had been before. And he had already been plenty compelling.

Well, it wasn't as if she hadn't seen the danger sign.

But Marlee decided, right then and there, she was giving up on her lifelong tendency toward caution.

She would *embrace* the cliff. She wouldn't fall. She would jump! Not her, precisely, but the woman drinking rum and contemplating the smoking of a cigar.

"This dress makes me want to get on a horse, pull a bandanna over my face and rob trains," she told him.

The smile that had been tickling the wickedly attractive curve of his mouth formed fully, revealing the full straightness of his teeth, as white as the towel around his neck.

Then he threw back his head and laughed. The column of his throat looked strong and touchable. The sound of his laughter was more intoxicating than the rum.

She, Marlee Copeland, had just made a very attractive man laugh. That felt like a cigarworthy reason for celebration!

"The cigar matches your start on your career as a criminal. People sometimes lick them before they light them."

"What?"

"They're usually wine-dipped."

She flicked the cigar with her tongue.

"Here," he said, gently. "Let me take that."

And just like that, his hand brushed hers, and a few more rocks crumbled from that cliff.

He took the cigar.

His eyes lingered on her lips.

A fire leaped to life within her.

"I wonder if there's really a wild, train-robbing outlaw under all that green fluffy stuff."

"It's not green." Her voice was hoarse, a choked whisper. "It's sea foam. Chiffon."

He held up the cigar and his tongue slipped out and licked it, exactly where her own tongue had been. His eyes were steady on hers. It was shockingly sensual.

"I need to get out of this scratchy dress," she said. What had made her say *that*? It was totally inappropriate. Did it sound as if she wanted to get out of the dress *with him*? Did it sound like an invitation?

Why did she always have to be so socially inept, blurting things out awkwardly?

Why did men like this always make her feel like a tongue-tied teenager?

Fiona had been right. This dress *did* suit her.

On the other hand, what would a train-robbing, cigar-loving, rum-drinking outlaw do? She could be that. For just a few minutes in time, she could. Maybe just for one night.

She took a deep breath. She felt as if she was on the edge of a cliff, trying to build up her nerve to jump.

"Want some company for your swim?" she asked. This was complete insanity. She was not a very good swimmer.

He tilted his head and regarded her, no doubt as surprised as she herself was.

Marlee's breath stopped in her chest. That was what you got for trying to break out of your mold, she thought, a little nervously.

A one-way trip off a cliff. The cigar, the rum, the remarks had made her feel as if she could be bold.

One thing she should remember about cliff jumps: as exhilarating as the ride down was, the landing was going to be bumpy. Painful.

He was going to think of a way to squirm out of it.

He needed to be alone. He'd had a hard day at work.

"Of course, I'd love for you to join me," he said.

A man like him—just like a dress like this—made her reconsider the kind of girl she had always been.

She was on a tropical island with a complete stranger. Why not let loose? Why not let down her hair? Did she really want to be the person that was looked at in a dress like this and heard the proclamation, *It's you.*

Marlee was not the kind of girl who went for moonlit swims with strange men. But what had she ever gotten out of life by being the kind of girl she was?

"Are you allowed to?" she blurted, realizing she was scrabbling for an exit.

He raised a questioning eyebrow at her.

"You know. Um, fraternizing with the guests. It's usually against the rules. Of a resort."

Sheesh. As if she was any kind of expert in resorts.

"You're right," he said, after a moment. "It usually is. But there's something about a cigar-holding woman that just brings out the outlaw in me, too."

She shivered. He was so sexy it felt as if she was swan-diving off that cliff, her arms flung open wide to a terrifying and exhilarating adventure where there was absolutely no way of predicting how or where she would fall.

CHAPTER THREE

SHE DIDN'T EVEN know his name and there was something thrilling and electrical leaping in the air between them.

Marlee was aware she was playing with the proverbial fire.

Still, she was on this island for five days for a wedding. Only three whole days if you took out the travel days. It felt as if the clock was ticking.

She could remake herself into anything she wanted to be.

Couldn't she?

She suddenly couldn't wait to rid herself of the dress and any remnant of the person she had always expected herself to be.

"I'll babysit the cigar while you go change." He put it to his lips again and took a leisurely taste of it. Even though it was not lit, the air was filled with sweet, smoky sensuality.

Unfortunately, there weren't many ways that could draw a woman's attention to a man's mouth more than that.

"Almost as good as a kiss," he decided, his

voice sultry and hot like the tropical night. "I can taste you on it."

As if this wasn't dangerous enough without kisses entering the discussion! She felt a deep sense of wanting to taste him.

And not through a shared, unlit cigar, either.

"I don't even know you name."

"Matteo," he offered. "And yours?"

"Marlee."

He bowed slightly. "The pleasure is mine."

Good grief! It was? *Matteo.* What a gorgeous, exotic name.

"I'll just be a sec," she croaked, and slipped through the open door of her cabana. Her heart was beating as hard as if she had just run a hundred-meter dash with a gold medal at stake.

Now what? She hoped good sense—something she was known for, which meant she probably deserved this dress—would return. But it did not.

Her cheeks felt hot. She hoped the darkness had hidden that from him.

Or did he suspect she was a little naive and not very worldly?

Still, here was the truth. She, Marlee Copeland, librarian from Seattle, was going to go for a midnight swim with a gorgeous, exotic man named Matteo. Was it midnight?

Who cared? It was just as he said. It was midnight somewhere. It was dark. It was com-

pletely against her nature to be so spontaneous, so throwing-caution-to-the-wind. Maybe
that was why it felt so absolutely exhilarating.

Marlee went through the darkened space of
her tiny cabana, not wanting to turn on a light.
What was that about? She was afraid the dream-
like quality of this experience could not hold up
to having a light shined on it, that's what.

That should have given her pause, but it didn't.
Instead, she found her suitcase, open on the bed,
and rummaged through it in the dark until her
hands found the slippery fabric of her swimsuit.

She ducked into the bathroom. Again, she was
reluctant to turn on the light, as if the fairy tale
would come to an end if exposed to light. Plus,
of course, she'd have to look at herself in her
swimsuit.

That would be enough to make her lose her
nerve.

Somehow, she got out of the dress and left it
in a rumpled pile on the floor. She wriggled into
the swimsuit. It was a one piece. It felt as if it
was binding. She knew she had gained a bit of
weight since her jilted-at-the-altar fiasco. Five
pounds. Maybe ten.

*That's why she had been earmarked for the
hideous dress. To artfully hide a few pounds so
she wouldn't wreck the wedding photos.*

Okay, so she wasn't sexy in a swimsuit. She

did not need any more sexiness than his presence already provided. And despite the cigar and the rum and saying yes to the invitation, she didn't want him to get the wrong idea.

Or did she?

Suddenly wrong and right and who decided these things seemed like terrible constraints to adventure and boldness and living life one hundred percent.

Was she really going to go for a swim with a stranger?

She came to her senses, just like that. She threw on the light. As she had suspected, the bathing suit did absolutely nothing for her. She looked like she had been stuffed into a sausage casing.

She looked extraordinarily plain, with her mousy, shoulder-length hair still travel-crumpled. Her green eyes had tired smudges under them. The bathing suit revealed way too much skin that had a certain lard-like shade to it. No wonder Fiona had suggested a few extra days in the sun!

In fact, Marlee thought she looked exactly like a person who spent their days in a library, carefully selecting wonderful books for the highlight of her week—story time!

She was the kind of person *that* dress was made for. The kind of person abandoned a week before their wedding because her fiancé had suddenly discovered the painful truth.

It was all too dull and unexciting for him.

Which she translated to mean *she* was too dull and unexciting for him.

For Arthur. Who had not exactly been a ball of fire himself.

She quickly gathered the dress off the floor and hung it over the shower bar. She took a deep breath, mourning the moment that almost had been. Then, Marlee wrapped a towel around herself, marched across the floor and poked her head out the door.

She could see him standing out there, his wide, naked back to the cabana. Matteo. What was that, exactly? Italian? They liked their women more on the voluptuous side, didn't they?

The words she was going to speak—*I've changed my mind, I've come to my senses*—froze inside her. She took a deep breath. They still didn't come out.

A voice inside her begged her to prove Arthur wrong.

Live.

For once, just live.

Marlee backed away from the door and returned to the suitcase. Tucked into a corner of it was the lingerie she had chosen for her own wedding night.

When she had packed it, she had told herself she was being practical. Why let it go to waste? The underwear—which had promised to be seamless—had been beautiful underneath her wedding gown. Why not use it with her bridesmaid's dress? Wouldn't those same seamless qualities be great for a day where she would be somewhat in the spotlight? Where she would be posing for pictures?

The reveal of the bridesmaid's dress really rendered all those reasons to use the underwear unnecessary. There were so many frills that an extra underwear line or two would hardly be noticeable!

Her hidden self, she thought, as she touched the exquisite lace on the matching white bra and panties.

Of course, when she had purchased them, she had done so in anticipation that someday her hidden self was going to be revealed to her delighted groom.

The saleslady had even shown her a quick release on the bra, saying, "To minimize the, er, awkward moments of your wedding night."

Marlee was so tired of being the good girl. She was so tired of living by the rules.

Yes. She would go for a midnight swim. With a sexy stranger. In her underwear, instead of her frumpy bathing suit. These days, and in the dark, who could possibly tell the difference?

Matteo waited on the darkened path in front of Marlee's cabana. The night was unbelievably beautiful: stars studding an inky dark sky, the air so soft and moist it felt like a touch, the waves whispering a timeless song. A nearby bird screeched loudly, and he caught sight of bright feathers through the waxy green foliage of palm trees.

He had not been to the tropics before, and standing here, in the utter enchantment of it, he wondered why.

Of course, how much of the enchantment was his chance encounter with her?

Marlee.

He was, he thought, misrepresenting himself just a bit. For some reason the cigar-wielding vision that had materialized on the pathway thought he worked at the resort.

She had been a surprise, tucked in among the foliage, fondling the cigar and drinking rum.

She said it was because of the dress, but it wasn't until she mentioned it that he had even noticed it.

Not when he was entranced by her eyes. They were as green and lustrous as jade. They were so compelling, now that he thought about it, he couldn't recall the color of her hair.

But he could imagine her lips: wide, plump, unglossed, and not in need of any kind of improvement, either.

There was something about her both understated and overstated, which made her an intriguing contradiction that begged exploring. She had the clear eyes of an angel, but she was debating corrupting those luscious lips by smoking a cigar and dreaming of robbing trains!

He increasingly lived in a highly predictable world. Everything was highly scheduled. Managed. Controlled.

He liked it that way.

But if he liked it so much, why was he so susceptible to the intrigues of a spontaneous encounter?

Maybe, Matteo admitted reluctantly, it was a distraction from that troubling thought he'd had looking at the brochure, which claimed Coconut Cay was the safest place on earth. His painful experience was that danger rarely came from outside sources.

He didn't want to think about that, revisit the pain of his mother's long illness and his brokenhearted father's terrible slide…

He deliberately avoided relationships deepening into the zone where they could cause that kind of cataclysmic destruction of a world.

He was a numbers man, and he had done the cost-benefit analysis. He had seen, firsthand, the terrible cost that could be extracted at the altar of love.

So, given all that, this distraction itself had the potential for danger, didn't it?

Not really. He was here for a few days. Tonight was his only free evening. There was, thankfully, no time for developments of the complicated romantic kind.

He was going for a swim. Period.

Because of the meteoric rise of the family business he had saved from near ruin, Matteo was a public figure now. He could not risk being politically incorrect, letting his guard down, not even for one playful moment.

As was so much these days, this forever being on guard was part of what made living life in the spotlight so tiresome.

He'd told Marlee he'd been working all day. That there had been some unexpected challenges. She had jumped to the conclusion that he'd been working *here*.

The truth was he'd been thirty thousand feet above the earth, in his private jet, working on a business issue so complicated and dull it had put him to sleep.

To be honest, he found it hard to envision what kind of unexpected challenges might arise in a place like Coconut Cay.

Still, he had not rushed to correct her, to assure her he would in no way be fraternizing with her.

The truth was he had *enjoyed* her not having a clue about who he was. Increasingly, and distressingly, in Europe he was recognized as the CEO of Monte Rosa Alpen. He'd recently been stopped, in downtown Zurich, by a French tourist who had wanted his autograph and a photo together!

But success wasn't just making him highly— and uncomfortably—recognizable by strangers.

It was changing the way people around him interacted with him.

Women, in particular, seemed besotted with what his success could mean to *them.*

And for all that the attention was flattering initially, Matteo found he had quickly become quite jaded. When was the last time he had been liked for himself, instead of being seen as an opportunity, an important connection, someone who could be *used?*

He was grateful for old friendships, the ones he had had since long before he had achieved such success.

Which was how he found himself on Coconut

Cay when he really didn't have the time right now to be here, and when this, despite its exotic beauty, wasn't his kind of place.

Or at least he had thought it wasn't. But now that he was here, he wasn't so sure.

He hadn't allowed himself the gift of downtime for as long as he could remember. He sometimes dreamed of the high and rugged places of his youth, far away from the pressures of his electronics and his life, but he did not indulge.

He was driven, absolutely and utterly. He had been consumed by a single mission. Saving the business that had been in his family for four hundred years.

No, there was no time for frivolities in Matteo's life. Even now, there was a sense that he could not let his guard down, that it all could slip away, as it had done for his father.

But when an old university friend—a friend who knew Matteo inside and out, and was unmoved by the fact he had graced the covers of business magazines or that he had been listed as one of the one hundred wealthiest people in the world—asked a favor, the answer was simply yes.

Because you knew that friend would do the same for you. And would do the same for you regardless of whether you were one of the richest men in the world, or down-and-out on a street corner somewhere.

The door whispered open behind him, and he turned.

Marlee appeared, and it seemed as if she might be dressed in only a towel!

CHAPTER FOUR

MATTEO'S MOUTH WENT DRY.

Though, now that he looked more carefully, he could see—thank goodness—narrow white bathing suit straps over her shoulders.

For some reason, the realization she had something on under the towel did not take away the dryness from his mouth.

He was not sure he had ever seen eyes as green as hers. In an environment that shimmered with a thousand enchanting shades of that color, her eyes put all else to shame.

They invited something in him to let go.

It felt as if his barriers dissolved completely. Instead of feeling terrifying, it felt freeing. For this one moment in time, he would accept the reprieve he had been granted from all his responsibilities and obligations.

Marlee's hair—the hair Matteo hadn't remembered because he was so entranced with her eyes—was light brown, and the moonlight played with that, spinning it into shades of gold.

Her feet and shoulders were bare, the skin of her shoulders milky white, but the moon played with that, too, and her skin seemed to be shimmering with silver.

Were those straps over her shoulders bathing suit straps, or was she in her underwear?

Matteo gulped. What, exactly, had he allowed into his well-ordered life? He set down the unsmoked cigar on a rock wall as if it was the problem, the reason he was in this predicament.

He, of all people, should know what a terrible path giving in to these kinds of temptations could take a man down.

They walked, in silence, to the beach. He was aware the scent of her was clean, fresh, unperfumed.

He had seen the beach from the plane earlier, but nothing could have prepared him for the astounding beauty of it at night. It was a crescent of pure white sand, surrounded by gently swaying palms. The foamy waves caressing the shore were, like her skin, spun to silver.

He hesitated. He recognized this as a jumping-off point. A choice to turn away from the organized life he had made for himself.

This encounter was ripe with opportunities for what Matteo liked least: the unexpected. Could he say to her he had made a mistake? Or that he didn't feel like swimming after all? Could he alter the course, right now, of what was about to happen? Did he want to?

He could feel her hesitation, too.

He turned and looked at her.

Her eyes captivated him, again. So many contradictions. How could she seem both bold and shy?

How could she seem both strong and fragile?

If he said, right now, he had changed his mind, he felt, intuitively, he would hurt her in some way and he could not do it.

He took the towel from his shoulders and dropped it to the sand. He was aware that his senses were intensely engaged: he could smell the sea, and Marlee. It felt as if he could feel each individual grain of sand beneath his feet.

And so, when the towel dropped from her, it was but a whisper, and yet, with his senses so heightened, it sounded like thunder in the distance.

He was afraid to look.

And he could not have stopped himself from looking. Not if his entire future and his entire fortune were on the line.

She was not dressed in a bathing suit.

She was dressed in a bra and panties, brilliantly white against the night darkness. They were heart-stoppingly skimpy and appeared to be constructed of mist and cobwebs. Marlee was a goddess of sensuality. Her creamy white skin—perfect—pebbled as the night air touched it.

Matteo thought of all his control, and how, even with all that, he could not have predicted the day ending like this, in a moment that shimmered and sizzled with her pure allure. Her femininity, the sweet curves of her, made him feel masculine. And strong.

And completely powerless at the same time.

As Matteo took her in, Marlee felt the air turn electric around them, as if a power line had broken and was whipping back and forth, snapping and cracking.

Her skin shivered with awareness as she contemplated the fact that she—Marlee Copeland, librarian—was on a beautiful beach, nearly naked in her wedding night lingerie, with a man she did not know.

It had to be a dream.

And if it was, she was making the most of it. The new her—the one that was surprisingly embracing this bold persona—laughed out loud and relished how Matteo's eyes darkened from turquoise to navy blue.

She broke the intensity and dashed by him.

"Race you to the water," she called over her shoulder.

They raced across the creamy, fine sand. Despite her lead, he surged ahead of her, but they reached the edge of the water together, and the shocking chilliness of the ocean would have stopped her dead, except he continued forward. When he realized she had lost momentum, he reached back, grabbed her hand and flung himself into water the color of black ink, drawing her in with him.

The water closed over her head. Choking, she found the sandy bottom with her feet, and she rose out of the water. It occurred to her she wasn't sure how transparent her underwear was when wet, so she ducked back down, squatting in the water, the sea lapping at her chin.

He was not so self-conscious. Well, why would he be? Marlee watched the water sluice off the beautiful lines of Matteo's sculpted chest. He looked just a little too pleased with himself, though, because he was such a fine male specimen, or because he had managed to duck her, she wasn't sure.

"Hey!" she scolded him. "I wanted to get in slowly."

He made chicken sounds. Because she wanted to get in slowly, or because she was up to her chin in water?

"I'm not a very good swimmer," she said.

He looked immediately contrite, and she took advantage and splashed him mightily.

He laughed and darted away from her before she could wind up and get him again. And the game was on. Soon, as they chased each other through the dark water, she lost all sense of self-consciousness. They ran and played until they were utterly breathless with laughter and exertion.

The resistance of the sea pulling on their thighs made it feel as if they were slogging through quicksand.

He was way stronger than her. Way faster. He could have easily outstripped her, but he was deliberately slowing down, teasing her, making her think he was within arm's reach, before putting on another burst of speed.

When he slowed again, with a mischievous, you-can't-catch-me glance over his broad shoulder, Marlee threw herself in his direction. She connected! Gleefully, she wrapped her arms around his waist and clung there. His skin was warm and slick, alive somehow, beneath her fingertips.

With a shout, he toppled, and as he splashed into the ocean, she let go of him, not feeling nearly as cautious of the water as she usually did. When Matteo rose out of the water, she was already running away from him.

She was laughing so hard she could not gain traction. She could feel him gaining on her, his breath hot on her neck. She tumbled down under a wave. He sliced in behind her, grabbed her foot and held while she came to the surface, stood on one leg and tried to kick free.

The water didn't feel cold anymore. It was now as warm and sensuous as his touch.

"I'm going to drown," she warned him, bouncing on one leg and splashing him. "From laughing."

"Ah," he said, not releasing her foot. "But what a way to go."

It would be a great way to go, Marlee decided. It felt as if she could drown on laughter. And joy. Freedom. When had she ever felt this free?

And then he took the captive foot and, his eyes locked on her face, he lifted it to his lips.

It still felt, again, as if she was going to drown, but suddenly not from laughing. Her laughter died. His lips touched her big toe, and then, shockingly, his tongue darted between her big toe and the next one.

The sensation was so strong it felt as if it could not be borne by something as inconsequential as a human being. Time stood still. Her every sense rippled and her every nerve tingled. She could see each drop of water as it slid through his hair, down his neck, caressed his bare, wet chest.

He let go of her foot, apparently as stunned with himself as she was.

She stared at his lips. She wanted desperately to taste him.

It occurred to Marlee that she had nearly married a man who had never once made her feel anything like what she was feeling now.

The earth shifting beneath her feet, the stars swirling in the inky night above her.

Earthquake.

Or maybe tsunami.

The playfulness seemed to be gone from the moment, but it had felt so much safer that she tried to restore what they had been seconds ago. She splashed him, hoping to somehow recapture their earlier mood. But the water caught at her legs and she went down. She swallowed water and floundered. She felt panic set in.

Then strong arms caught her, lifted her to her feet. She leaned into him and sputtered as he pounded her back.

Finally, she got her breath and took a step away from him.

"I think I might live," she croaked.

"Uh," he said, "Marlee?"

She nodded, licked her lips. How could her mouth feel so dry with all this water around them?

"You seem to have, um, lost something."

She tilted her head toward him. She was aware she had indeed lost something. Her sanity. And it was the most blissful loss of her life.

"Your bathing suit top," he said, his voice a hoarse whisper.

She dropped her head and felt the absolute shock of it. Obviously her quick-release wedding night bra was not made for strenuous water play. The magic drained from the moment like air from a needle-pricked balloon.

She squealed, folded her arms around herself and sank down in the water to her neck.

"Don't look!" she ordered him.

"Um, okay."

But he was still looking!

"Stop it!"

"Okay," he said. He held up his hands in surrender and turned away from her.

Not trusting him at all, Marlee duckwalked toward shore, and when she was close enough, she rose and sprinted. Utterly mortified, she practically catapulted from the water and up the beach to where her towel was. She grabbed it, wrapped it around herself and raced for the safety of her cabana.

That had been just a little too *free*.

She did not look back. She did not want to see his embarrassed expression. In fact, Marlee hoped with all her heart that she would never see Matteo again.

This was a lesson for her: she was not the carefree kind of girl.

She was not the woman who could let go of control and experience no consequences. She was not the bandanna-wearing-bandit type.

It had been an experiment and it had failed. She should never have let go of who she really was.

And she never would again.

Never.

Considering how humiliating the experience had been, she expected embarrassment might keep her up all night. Instead, she slept deeply and dreamlessly and woke up ravenous. When she looked at herself in the mirror in the morning, she expected to look as if she had a hangover.

But even though her hair was a mess from sleeping on it wet, her eyes had a shocking glow to them. Her appearance really suggested more had happened than chasing each other through the sea and losing her top.

Marlee tossed on a sweat suit and a pair of dark glasses, and pulled a ball cap low over her eyes. Although satisfied that her disguise would keep her from being recognized for the underwear-clad nymph who had played in the water, or for a cigar-holding, rum-swilling bandito, she kept a wary eye out for a certain hotel employee in case she had to duck behind a palm tree to avoid an encounter.

Marlee made her way to the resort restaurant, marveling at how the early-morning sun made the sweat suit seem as if she was overdressed already.

The resort had a different feel in the bright morning light. The thick foliage lining the curving paths rioted with kaleidoscopes of flowers whose scents tickled her nostrils and perfumed the air. Sparkling white villas and cabanas were nearly completely hidden by thick greenery, even if they were only steps from the path.

The path opened to the pool, blue waters mirrorlike. Navy-striped lounge chairs underneath huge, taupe-colored umbrellas were scattered around it. Off to one side of the pool was the main dining center and a cluster of quaint, partially open-air shops that specialized in resort must-haves: everything from books to snorkels to swimsuits. A bright yellow sundress caught the breeze in front of one of them and danced, flirting with her.

Ignoring its temptations, she entered the restaurant. Marlee lifted her sunglasses and let her eyes adjust to the sudden dimness. The dining facility was utterly gorgeous, displaying an eclectic mix of antique cane furniture and amazing portraits of local island people.

Still, she mustn't let her curiosity and her love of such things get her guard down. She took a furtive look around and settled her sunglasses on the brim of her ball cap. She quickly filled a plate at the buffet, intending to take it back to her room. She was starving. She hadn't eaten at all last night.

"Marlee! There you are!" Fiona came through the doors and sailed over to her, a battleship on a mission.

"You didn't come to the pool last night," she said accusingly.

"I'm sorry. I was exhausted. I fell asleep."

Marlee was a little shocked by how easily the lie tripped off her lips. However, the truth—that she had been playing in the sea with a handsome stranger—was more likely to seem like a fib to the woman who had chosen *that* dress for her.

Fiona regarded her with very real concern. "You're not sick, are you?"

"I hope not."

"Because that would throw a real wrench into the wedding."

Marlee looked at her friend and felt as if she was seeing something she had never seen before.

Not about her friend. Fiona was just Fiona.

But about herself. And what she had accepted in life, from a fiancé who would abandon her at the altar, to a friend who was more concerned about appearances than her friend's well-being.

That was the problem with experiencing life the way Marlee had experienced it last night.

Yes, it had been brief.

But she had been so on fire with life. So engaged. So joyous. So uncontrolled. So free.

A person was changed by that.

No matter how badly the unfortunate consequences made them want to leave it behind them.

"Look," Fiona said. "I want to show you something."

She pulled her phone out of her pocket and held it up to Marlee. A woman in a beautiful bridal gown was kissing the nose of a wide-eyed foal.

"Isn't that the best wedding picture ever?" Fiona asked dreamily.

"Um…" Marlee said. She was aware yesterday she would have just demurred. Sure. Best wedding photo ever.

But she could feel a shift in her. "I guess I don't really see the relevance."

Fiona tsked. "*You* wouldn't. Anyway, eat up." She took a sudden interest in Marlee's plate. "Goodness, all those carbs!"

And the carb addict had been cavorting in the sea with the world's most attractive man last night. Perhaps losing her top hadn't even been the most embarrassing part of the evening. Her wedding lingerie! And the extra bulges from mourning her canceled wedding. Madness.

Marlee thought of Matteo's lips on her foot and shivered, felt again some shift inside.

This time she was annoyed with herself. She and Fiona had been friends since the fifth grade. You didn't start looking at your friends with a critical eye because a strange man had kissed your foot!

"Please don't be sick!" Fiona instructed her. "I've made spa appointments for this afternoon. Pedicures. Matching toenails for all of us! Won't that make a great wedding photo? Not as good as the baby horse, of course, but still."

Despite her desire not to be critical of her friend, Marlee bit her tongue to prevent herself from asking if Fiona planned to have Mike, the groom, in any of her wedding photos.

The door to the restaurant swung open.

Oh no! Marlee felt panicked. It was Matteo. He looked even more gorgeous in the light of day then he had last night. She felt paralyzed.

He wasn't in the tidy gray uniform the hotel staff wore. In fact, he looked exceedingly casual in a patterned button-down shirt, pressed khaki shorts, and sandals.

His hair was wet. He must have just showered.

He looked effortlessly sexy.

Move, she ordered herself while Fiona was distracted by him. Well, what woman wouldn't be?

The man had seen her bare breasts! She certainly didn't want him to see her crumpled, pale pink sweat suit or her plate full of carbs!

She yanked the sunglasses down and pulled the cap low over her eyes. She set down her food on the nearest table, never mind the looks of the astonished people dining there.

Marlee looked desperately for an exit that would not take her anywhere near him. She saw one and slunk toward it.

CHAPTER FIVE

ALMOST THERE. MARLEE just had to squeeze behind that warming tray full of scrambled eggs and then—

"Oh my!" Fiona squealed. "Matt!"

Marlee froze and watched in horror as Fiona raced across the room and enveloped Matteo in a hug as if he were her long-lost friend. Then, the bride-to-be turned and scanned the room.

Marlee's hand was on the door. She hoped it wasn't one of those exits that was for emergency use only.

She pressed down on the lever and allowed relief to sweep her when no alarm went off as the door swung open a crack. The relief was short-lived.

"Marlee," Fiona cried, "come here! You must meet our best man."

What? No! Matteo was *not* their best man. Their best man's name was Matt. It was somebody Mike had gone to college with. They'd been roommates.

Still, she lost that precious opportunity to

make good her escape as she grappled with the fact that Fiona knew Matteo.

Fiona was gesturing her over.

Run, Marlee ordered herself.

She let the door close with herself still on the inside of it. If they were all in the same wedding party—and apparently they were—why put off this horrible reunion?

With one last forlorn look at the exit, Marlee reluctantly shuffled across the room.

"Marlee, this is Matt Keller, our best man," Fiona gushed. "Marlee is one of my bridesmaids. I've been telling her all about you, haven't I, Marlee?"

Yes, indeed she had.

Mike's best man, his friend from college, had gone on to become some kind of international tycoon who regularly front-covered all the European business magazines. Fiona seemed to regard someone of his reputation and fame being part of the wedding party as a personal coup.

"We've met," Marlee said awkwardly. She glanced into those turquoise eyes. She was pretty sure they were dancing with mirth. She took interest in the buffet. She didn't offer her hand.

"You have?" Fiona stammered. "But how is that—"

"Barely," Matteo said smoothly, and Marlee

shot him a look. A little smile was tickling the gorgeous line of those lips. Those lips that had touched her toes ever so briefly.

Marlee could feel a blush rising in her cheeks. Still, she tilted her chin bravely and gave him a narrow-eyed look of warning.

"I found the suit you left me," Matteo said to Fiona without looking at Fiona at all. His eyes, brimming with laughter, were intense on Marlee's face. "Double-breasted."

Her face felt incredibly hot, like it might catch fire. She prayed Fiona would not notice.

"What?" Fiona said. "It was not! Double-breasted? That would be a disaster."

"Not at all," Matteo said smoothly. "I quite liked it."

Marlee felt as if she would like to kick his shin to wipe that smug look off his face.

Fiona's voice rose shrilly. "Please tell me they didn't deliver the wrong suit. I'm not sure it could be fixed at this point. I'm finding out it's very hard to get things here."

"Come to think of it, I don't think it was double-breasted," Matteo said, apparently taking pity on the misery he was causing poor Fiona by having a laugh at Marlee's expense. "I'm just preoccupied."

If his eyes dropped to what he was preoccupied with, Marlee thought she would probably die. But they didn't. They remained steadfast on hers.

"Of course you are, Matt," Fiona cooed. "Such a large company! But if you could check the suit as soon as possible. I'm panicking!"

"I will. No need to panic." He still did not take his eyes off Marlee. She tilted her chin a little higher at him.

Fiona shot a look between Matteo and Marlee. She frowned suspiciously. Marlee could see Fiona didn't really like it that Matteo was focused on Marlee and not her. She whipped out her phone.

"I was just showing Marlee this picture. What do you think?"

Marlee caught a glimpse of the bride-with-foal shot before Matteo took the phone and squinted thoughtfully at it.

"Interesting," he said, his attention turned briefly to Fiona's phone.

"It won the bride photo of the year."

Matteo turned his attention back to Marlee. He lifted an eyebrow. He might as well have spoken, their thoughts were so close.

Who knew there was a bride photo of the year?

Fiona drew in a breath. "There must be horses here on Coconut Cay. There must be! I bet if I can find a horse, the photographer could replicate this shot."

Marlee didn't want to lengthen this encounter by pointing out to Fiona that replicated shots probably had little chance of becoming a bride photo of the year.

"Isn't that odd?" Matteo said smoothly. "I know someone else who was looking for a horse. And a bandanna, and a train to rob."

Fiona looked at him, bewildered.

"Well," Marlee said brightly. "I was just leaving—"

"How hard could it be to find a horse?" Fiona asked. "Matteo, could you do it?"

He lifted a shoulder. "I doubt it. I'm not familiar with this place."

Now it was Marlee's turn to feel her mouth quirking upward. "Of course he could find a horse," Marlee said. "How hard could it be?"

He scowled at her. "I barely found the beach last night."

"Mike says you're totally a genius," Fiona said. "That you can do anything."

"Finding a photogenic horse will be child's play for you," Marlee could not resist adding.

His look darkened. He looked exceedingly sexy with that sinister look on his face.

"So that's settled," Fiona said with relief. "Thank you, Matt."

He looked slightly stunned. Marlee smirked.

"This morning? Please?"

Marlee's satisfied grin turned into a snicker, which she tried to suffocate. A mistake, as it drew Fiona's attention to her.

"Marlee, you go with him."

"What? No. I—"

"I mean, he's a businessman. The artistic aspects of it would probably be totally lost on him."

"The artistic aspects of finding a horse?" Matteo muttered.

"Exactly the problem," Fiona said. "It's not *any* horse. It's a baby horse. Not a white one, though, I don't want it to disappear in my dress."

"Now, *that* would make a photo," Matteo said, deadpan.

Marlee stifled another giggle.

"I meant the horse needs to contrast with my dress," Fiona clarified, annoyed. She looked between them. "That's the part I'm trusting you with, Marlee. You're very artistic. Remember the time you turned the library into a medieval castle for—"

"The library?" Matteo asked, arching one surprised eyebrow upward.

"Marlee's a librarian."

"A librarian," Matteo said, and the eyebrow went up even further.

"Actually, I can't remember why you turned the library into a castle," Fiona said, tapping her lip thoughtfully with one finger.

"King Arthur Days," Marlee said, a bit tightly. There. She was completely unmasked. Though after her quick exit from the water last night, Matteo had probably already figured out she wasn't really any kind of a wild outlaw.

She was a nerdy girl.

"I'm not asking too much, am I?" Fiona asked with a soft flutter of her lashes at Matteo.

Yes, Marlee thought, *she is.*

"Of course not," Matteo said evenly, seeming to have put away his reluctance for the task. He winked at Marlee. "We will make it our sacred mission."

We?

Marlee was not sure it was safe to think about sacred missions with a man like this.

"Won't we?" he prodded her. "Get abreast of this request, immediately?"

"I had something to do this morning," Marlee said.

"Nonsense," Fiona said dismissively. "Matteo, just make sure Marlee's back in time for pedicures."

He looked pointedly at Marlee's sandal-clad feet. She remembered the feel of his mouth on her toes.

This was the problem with giving up your customary inhibitions. Now, when she should have been shaking his hand and saying, *Nice to meet you*, she was thinking of his mouth on her toes.

"Two o'clock, for the pedicures," Fiona said, "And Matt, please check the suit. Can you take a picture of it and send it to me?"

"I will," Matteo promised.

"I'd love to stay and chat," Fiona said, "but I can't. I'm just going to grab a fruit plate—"

Did she send Marlee a look? Had she shoved them together on this sacred mission on purpose? Was Fiona matchmaking?

It seemed unlikely, since she was so preoccupied with her wedding.

"—and go to my meeting with the floral arranger. She doesn't think she can get gardenias!"

And then Fiona was gone and they stood looking at each other.

"A librarian," he said, tilting his head at her, obviously seeing her in a new light. "I suspected, from your reaction to a little wardrobe malfunction, you were not a rum-swigging, cigar-loving outlaw after all."

"I never said I was. I said that dress made me *want* to be."

"A librarian exploring her wilder side," he said softly, "Ooh-la-la. Take off your glasses for me."

She realized he was teasing her and that she was still wearing her sunglasses.

She took them off.

"Oh, my heart," he said, and placed his hands over it and staggered backward.

Did he have to be so effortlessly irresistible? She leveled him a look.

"You should have also told me who you were last night," she said.

"I did!" He moved past her to the buffet and took a plate. He was, she noted, a protein guy. Lots of eggs and bacon.

"You let me believe you were an Italian hotel employee," she said, picking her plate off the table where she had left it. She followed him as he took a seat. She sank into the one across from him.

"I never said I was a hotel employee."

"I assumed. Since you said you had been working all day. You could have fessed up when I asked you if it was against the rules for you to fraternize."

"I had been working all day. On my jet."

His jet? She was sitting across the table from a man with a jet. A man with a jet had tasted her toes last night.

"Plus, I never said I was Italian."

"The name sounded Italian to me."

"We do border Italy," he pointed out mildly.

"You had a million opportunities to tell me

who you really were, and did not," she said primly.

"Maybe not a million."

She leveled a look at him.

"Uh-oh," he said, "is that the quiet-in-the-library look?"

"No, it's the I-don't-believe-your-dog-ate-your-homework look."

He laughed. She shouldn't have found it nearly as satisfying as she did. Then, he was suddenly solemn.

"I did play along with your misconception," he confessed. "Sometimes it's exhausting being me. You don't have any idea how precious privacy is until people start recognizing you. I was so relieved that you didn't know who I was."

So now she felt ever so slightly sympathetic to one of the richest men in the world.

"Huh," she said, her sympathy feeling like a weakness, "if you want to be liked for who you are, maybe you shouldn't announce you have your own jet so soon after meeting someone."

His lips twitched. She couldn't tell if he was amused or annoyed.

"I can see there will be no winning with you, since you're equally irritated by me not telling you who I am *and* me telling you who I am. And meanwhile, you harbor a few contradictions of your own. Librarian or outlaw?"

"I'm all done exploring my wild side," she told him firmly. "Look at how that turned out."

CHAPTER SIX

MATTEO SMILED AT HER, a smile that was bone-meltingly sexy. "I thought it turned out rather amazingly," he said.

"It was mortifying. And it's particularly insensitive of you to not see that and to continue making jokes about it."

There! Exactly what an uptight librarian would say.

"Don't be embarrassed about last night," he said quietly, suddenly serious. "Please."

"Does that mean you've run out of puns?"

"Oh, no, I could come up with dozens more of those."

"Please don't! They aren't funny."

"And that's the naked truth."

She wanted to remain uptight. Prim. For the first time in her life, Marlee wondered if that was a persona she hid behind.

Hid what? she asked herself, appalled. She thought of his lips on her toes. She frowned at him to hide the shiver that went up and down her spine.

"Okay, okay," Matteo said, holding up his

hands, as if in surrender. "I'll try to be sensitive. Why are Americans so uptight, anyway? Most of the people in the world enjoy beaches without their tops on."

And he would probably know, because he, sophisticated, star businessman that he was, had probably visited all kinds of beaches like that!

"Speaking of which, I have something that belongs to you."

He took a crumpled wisp out of his front pant pocket and dangled it in front of her.

"Is this your idea of sensitive, waving my underwear around in public?" Marlee hissed at him in an undertone.

"I'm not waving it. But I could."

He gave her a mischievous look. She grabbed her bra—still damp—from him and stuffed it in her own pocket.

"I'll work on sensitivity," he promised. "I'll work on it the whole time we go in search of the horse."

Save your dignity, Marlee told herself. *Wriggle out of this.*

But he was being so charming. How could anyone resist that playful expression?

And really, logically, wasn't the damage already done? It was not as if it could get any more embarrassing.

And they were going to run into each other.

They were both members of the same wedding party. They might as well get along, develop some comfort with each other.

It would make for better wedding photos if she wasn't glaring at him.

That was the logical explanation. The illogical part was that she *wanted* to be with him. Why? It could go nowhere.

They were obviously from different stratospheres.

But there was also an appeal in that. It could go nowhere. She was only going to be on this island for a few days.

She was newly single, and definitely sworn off the complexities of relationships, anyway. There didn't have to be an agenda all the time. She didn't always have to be the uptight librarian, weighing every option, considering the future. It was marvelously freeing, if you thought about it.

Why not enjoy her time here on Coconut Cay, and by extension, Matteo? He was smart and funny, not to mention attractive. She could have fun. She could! People were always talking about being in the moment.

Last night she had experienced that. It was an elixir that made you want more.

Matteo sat outside the resort gate waiting for Marlee and enjoying the warmth of the sun, so different than the Zurich experience at this time of year.

He had come from the airport by limo last night, through a different entrance, and was now surprised to see the pedestrian access to the resort actually opened onto a chaotic main street of the village of Charlee.

The narrow, cobblestoned street was swarming with morning activity. Buildings, plastered in pastel shades and filled with crowded shops, seemed to lean in toward it. The noise, colors and scents were in such sharp contrast to his own villa that it seemed almost as if the resort was tucked behind a cloister wall.

His observations stopped as Marlee came out the gate. His focus narrowed to just her.

She was carrying a large purse and had on a yellow sundress, the antithesis of that dress she'd had on last night and the horrible velour number she'd had on at breakfast.

While the dress wasn't quite as sexy as her bathing attire, it was decidedly daring, with its spaghetti straps and short, swirly skirt.

She looked darned uncomfortable about it, too, and for some reason her discomfort was endearing.

A breeze chose that moment to lift the hem, showing off the long length of her legs. She tried, unsuccessfully, to pin the dress in place with her arms.

She glared at him when she saw him grinning at her. Arms still holding the dress down, she shuffled over to where he was parked at the curb.

"What the heck is this?" Marlee asked.

"It's a scooter," Matteo said, straddling the two-wheeler he'd rented.

"Clearly it's a scooter," she said, annoyed. She looked down at herself.

She wasn't dressed for a scooter.

It was truly refreshing that she had no idea she was the goddess she had revealed to him last night.

"Sorry," he said. "It turns out transportation options are limited on the island. There are two cabs, both taken. I went online and found the name of a stable, but it's not within walking distance."

"Oh."

"Did you want to go change?" he asked sympathetically.

She considered this, and him. She took a deep breath, like someone about to leap off a cliff.

"No, I'll be fine," she said.

"Okay." He patted the seat behind him, and she slid onto it. Amazingly, given how small the seat was, he could have inserted a travel trunk between the two of them. She put her purse in the space.

"What do I hang on to?" she asked. "There doesn't seem to be any handles back here."

His mouth felt quite dry. The exact same way it had felt when her bathing suit had surrendered itself to the sea.

"Scooters don't come with handles. You hang on to me," he said. "You might want to move your purse."

There was a long silence. Her purse was moved over her shoulder and her hands crept to his sides, and rested there lightly, tentatively. How could that possibly feel so sexy? And it was about to get worse.

"Uh, I think you might have to hold on tighter than that."

"Now, that sounds like some kind of Italian playboy scheme," she said suspiciously.

"I am not a playboy."

"You have a jet. I'm not sure you need many qualifications beyond that."

"And I told you I'm not Italian. Anyway, suit yourself."

"I will."

He gave the scooter some gas. It spurted forward, and Marlee squealed and wrapped her arms around him.

"You did that on purpose," she accused him.

"I didn't. That wouldn't be sensitive. It's been years since I was on a motorbike."

"Jets will do that to a man," she said. "Make them give up their cheaper forms of transport. Don't go too fast."

Which, naturally, made him want to go faster. The next little spurt to get them into traffic might have been on purpose, but he was the one who suffered for it. Her arms wrapped tighter around him, snugging her right up against his back. Those long legs formed a warm V around him.

What kind of strange turn in his well-ordered life was this? Sharing a scooter with an unbelievably sexy woman in search of a horse?

This had not been his plan for this morning at all.

In case he ran into the mystery woman from last night he had intended to be cool.

To let her know he wasn't usually the type of man who cavorted in the sea with strangers.

To not let her know that a mere glimpse of her moon-gilded breasts had kept him awake most of the night thinking of how cool he would be next time he saw her!

But he might as well accept it.

Nothing on Coconut Cay was going to go according to his plan.

This morning being a prime example. He

hadn't expected to see her, and he hadn't expected to feel so protective of her when she was so clearly embarrassed about what had happened. How could you be cool in the face of that?

How could you express regret when you had no regrets?

So maybe it was her—Marlee, librarian-slash-outlaw—who threw a wrench into a man's carefully planned life.

Because here he was, going in search of a horse, of all things, and sharing a scooter with the goddess from the sea in a way he couldn't ignore how she stirred him physically.

He should have said no to Fiona. He should be working.

There was always work to do and it was always the antidote to any kind of uncomfortable feeling.

He glanced back at Marlee again, felt her physical closeness to him. Something unfolded in his gut.

"Keep your eyes on the road," she snapped. Then a squeal and "Watch out!"

"I saw her," he said, screeching to a halt that threw Marlee, impossibly, even harder against him.

A ruffled hen glared at him, clucked indignantly and guided her brood of chicks across the road in front of them.

Marlee giggled. Her breath was warm in his ear and he realized how glad he was that he wasn't working.

"I'm going to relax now," she told him firmly.

"Would you?"

With lots of stops and starts—and with near collision with a donkey cart—they finally made it out of the twisted, cobbled streets of the colorful town center.

The main road—it wasn't quite a highway—curved in and out of jumbled neighborhoods of humble but cheery houses with bright, painted doors and shutters and overflowing, flower-filled window boxes. Those districts gave way to ritzy residential areas built onto steep, green hills to capitalize on stunning views. The road meandered through dense vegetation, wound up steeply, hugged the edges of cliffs and then plummeted back down toward the sea.

It was all quite hair-raising, and after having to swerve around a pig napping in the middle of the road, Matteo declared it was time for a break. He pulled over at a roadside café that claimed to make the most famous iced coffee on the island.

They ordered coffee and sat at an outdoor table, chickens pecking around their feet as they admired the view that looked out over the Atlantic. Several other islands were visible in the distance. Matteo consulted his phone for a map to the stables.

"I think we should have been there by now," he said. He couldn't get a signal. He didn't want to tell Marlee, but he was pretty sure they were lost. How did you get lost on an island with one main road?

Marlee looked beautiful, her hair tangled, her face glowing from wind and sun. She did, indeed, look relaxed. She lifted a bare shoulder. "We'll find it. How hard can it be?"

He took a sip of the coffee. His eyes crossed. He pushed it away. "I think the famous coffee might be laced with the famous rum," he said.

She tasted hers. "Oh, yum," she said, and took a generous sip.

"I think your shoulders are getting burned," he said.

"That will never do! Think of the wedding photos." And then she snickered. Could the rum work that fast? He didn't think so.

In between sips of coffee—she had finished hers and started on his—she rummaged around in that big bag and found a tube of sunscreen. He glared down at his phone rather than watch her apply sunscreen to her shoulders. Maybe the rum was working that fast, because unless he was mistaken, she was being deliberately tantalizing about it.

"Can you check my back?"

He could hardly refuse, could he? He took the tube from her hand and got up from the table. He went behind her.

She lifted her hair off her neck, and he looked at the slender column of it and wanted to taste it. What was it about her that made him want to taste her?

He thought of how he'd lifted her toes to his mouth last night.

Stop it, Matteo ordered himself. Her skin, so delicate, was already starting to burn. Steeling himself to be a first aid man only, he slathered the cream onto her skin.

The minx closed her eyes, tilted her face to the sun and leaned into his fingertips.

He capped the tube, tossed it back at her and headed for the scooter. "Let's go," he called.

If he had hoped for a distraction from the sensation of her skin beneath his fingertips, he'd hoped in vain. She melted against him and he could feel her cheek on his back.

"Let's pretend," she suggested gleefully. "You're an Italian beach bum, and I'm an outlaw pretending to be a librarian."

He was going to say, *Let's not*, but he glanced over his shoulder. Her face had a light on in it—playful, invigorated, alive—that would take a man much stronger than him to put out.

He had the awful feeling she wasn't drunk on rum, but on life, and it was unbelievably appealing.

"I've never been on a motorbike before," she called.

"Calling it a motorbike is a bit of a stretch," he called back to her. "It's a scooter."

"Whatever it is, it's awesome. Go faster!"

He thought they were probably at about maximum speed already—in every single way—but if he could squeeze a little more power out of the machine, did that mean she would cling harder? He couldn't help himself. He had to find out.

And just like that, it *was* awesome: the wind, the sun, the charms of the island, a beautiful woman clinging to him. Matteo did something he rarely did.

He surrendered to the day.

He was pretty sure he was lost in more ways than one.

CHAPTER SEVEN

MARLEE WAS WELL aware she was flirting with a wilder side. It had started with the impulse buy of the bright yellow sundress this morning.

It was not the type of thing she *ever* bought. Loudly colored. Sexy. Flirty. Way too short.

But then again, she was not the type who swam in the sea with a stranger, either.

Or rode scooters.

Or invited men to apply sunscreen on her.

But something about breaking all these rules—doing what she had never even pictured herself doing, ever—was making her feel as if joy was shimmering inside her.

Okay, maybe the coffee *had* had rum in it, but Marlee felt intoxicated on life. It probably spoke to a life not well lived that this day, so far, felt like one of the highlights of her entire existence.

She was actually sorry when Matteo doubled back and found a worn sign that pointed down a rutted road to the stable.

The "stable" turned out to be a rickety lean-to with a palm frond roof.

And there was not a horse in sight.

Three tiny donkeys were saddled, and their owner introduced himself as Mackay and welcomed them with gregarious hopefulness.

Matteo explained their mission. Mackay's face fell.

"There are no horses on Coconut Cay," he said. "It's all donkeys."

"Not a single horse on the whole island?" Marlee asked.

"They eat too much," Mackay said. "The donkeys are better here."

Marlee considered this in terms of Fiona's request.

"They are cute," she said, moving over to one of the donkeys and rubbing his head. His friend, jealous, brayed loudly. She laughed and went to scratch his head, too.

"Do you think Fiona would be flexible?" she asked Matteo.

"On our short acquaintance I would guess, no, but you know her better than me."

"Hmm, I guess I'd say no."

"On the other hand," Matteo pointed out, "They are equines, aren't they? Same family?"

She felt doubtful. "It's a bit like calling a scooter a motorbike. A stretch."

"Here's to stretching," Matteo said.

She turned to Mackay. "I don't suppose you have a baby one?"

Mackay sadly shook his head no.

"They look like babies, even though they aren't," Matteo said, "And they aren't white, they're gray. And that one has black ears. That's three out of three checked on Fiona's list—equine, kind of a baby, not white."

"I think that's why I was sent along. For a guy, it's just a checklist. I'm in charge of the esthetics of the thing. But it's true," Marlee said, "the cute factor is off the scale."

"I think we have to make an executive decision. We've been given an assignment. We have a time crunch. Today's Thursday. The wedding is Saturday. Why don't we book one, and then we've got our bases covered? I'll take a picture and if Fiona vetoes it, that's okay. We did our best. Mackay, would one of the donkeys be available for a wedding on the weekend?"

Mackay puffed up as if one of his children had just won first prize at the spelling bee. "It would be my honor."

They worked out delivery details and gave him instructions to arrive shortly after the wedding for the photos.

"Which one would you like?" Mackay asked giving each donkey an affectionate rub on the head as he introduced them. "Henri, Harvey, Calamity."

"Let's eliminate Calamity just for the name," Marlee suggested.

Matteo inspected the two remaining donkeys with such a pretense of seriousness that she could not help laughing. "This one has the best ears," he decided.

"But look how hopeful that one looks!" she said, the laughter still bubbling.

"Okay," Matteo agreed. "This one."

"Henri, a fine choice," Mackay said with approval as if they had picked a great wine.

Matteo looked at his watch. "Our wedding assignment is completed. And before lunch! Which brings me to the topic of lunch. Are you hungry?"

"Starving," she said, and it was true, despite her carb-loaded breakfast.

"Can you recommend a place for lunch?" Matteo asked.

Mackay preened. "I have a lunch special today! I will take you to a secret beach. Very romantic."

"Oh." Marlee could feel herself blushing. She looked everywhere but at Matteo. "We're not, um, romantically involved."

Mackay looked between them, clearly disappointed. "Maybe by after lunch!" he said.

Matteo wagged wicked eyebrows at her, clearly enjoying her discomfort. "Here's to stretching," he said.

"Here's to sensitivity," she said.

He laughed.

"I don't think we have time," Marlee said. There was, thankfully, no time for *stretching*. Certainly not for romance.

Thank God.

"I have an appointment at two," she said.

"Only an hour!" Mackay promised. "Delicious lunch. Island cuisine, made by my mother."

"Made by his mother," Matteo said persuasively.

How could she resist this?

"It's only just gone noon," Matteo told her. "What do you say?"

And so she found herself perched in a sundress on the donkey named Henri, following Matteo, who was mounted on Calamity. Matteo should have looked hilarious, his long legs nearly on the ground, but instead Marlee found herself loving how he had embraced what the moment offered them. Not to mention loving the view of his broad back.

They rode a rutted trail with a lime grove on one side and a cliff on the other. The views out to the sea were spectacular, as was the scent of the limes. The sun kissed her face and a faint breeze lifted her hair.

It was bliss. No other description would do.

Mackay led the way on Harvey, down a steep, cliff-hugging trail. The stones that they knocked off the path seemed to clatter for a very long time before they hit the ground far below.

She would normally be a nervous wreck, but somehow she wasn't. The sense of bliss continued. It must be that rum-laced coffee!

The trail leveled out, and twisted through mangroves, opening up to the most beautiful beach Marlee had ever seen, the fine sand a pink as subtle as a young girl's blush.

Mackay spread a blanket on the sand and unpacked lunch from huge baskets. The cuisine was unbelievably good. It consisted of a jerk chicken, an amazing salad and a selection of island-grown fruits. Mackay produced a bottle of the local wine. Matteo refused because he was driving, but Marlee had some. It was foolish—she'd already had the rum-laced coffee—but what the heck? She'd never really been foolish before. She was quite enjoying it!

"Swim," Mackay insisted as he put lunch away. "The water is beautiful."

"I don't have a—"

"Not required here. I won't look," Mackay promised with a wink. "Henri might, though."

He shot Matteo a look that was loaded with male kinship. Their host was determined to get a romance going.

It was Matteo's turn to look uncomfortable. Considering he was familiar with sophisticated beaches around the world, he had a deer-caught-in-the-headlights look.

"I'd love to have a swim," Marlee decided. When had she ever felt this relaxed, this go-with-the-flow, this spontaneous?

She'd only had two glasses of wine. It wasn't that.

Matteo looked at her, then looked at his watch and yelped. "It's after one. We can't today."

Did she hear just a bit of relief in his voice at the time constraint? Marlee felt the sharpness of regret. On the other hand, if they got back in the water together, who was to say what could unfold between them? She thought of his lips on her toes. The look in his eyes when she had risen out of the water topless.

Maybe they would end up lovers!

That had to be the wine whispering to her, and still the possibility shivered up and down her spine. She was getting into deep water. She needed to remember she barely knew how to swim!

Matteo seemed suddenly extraordinarily eager to go, and helped Mackay pack up the baskets. In moments, the donkeys plodded their sure-footed way back up the cliff and to the stable. They got off and said goodbye to their host.

Matteo paid Mackay and gave him a tip that made him grin from ear to ear. Marlee kissed Henri right on the tip of his soft, beautiful nose.

And then they turned to where they had left the scooter. Matteo looked in shocked disbelief at the now empty space.

"It appears we've had a theft," he said.

"No, no," Mackay assured him. "Not stolen. Not on Coconut Cay."

"It's missing," Matteo pointed out. "I parked it right here."

"Borrowed, maybe," Mackay conceded.

"Borrowed, certainly," Matteo said. "The result is the same. We are left without a means to get back to the resort."

"I am without a vehicle today," Mackay said, but then brightened. "We can ride the donkeys to the main road, and from there you'll be able to make your way back to the resort."

"Make our way how?" Matteo asked skeptically.

"There's a bus," Mackay told them, "twice a day."

"I don't suppose I'm going to be back at the resort by two, am I?"

"Just stick out your thumb if you don't want to wait for the bus," Mackay said. "Someone will give you a ride."

"Hitchhike?" Marlee asked.

"Very safe here," Mackay promised.

"Uh-huh," Matteo said. "Safest place on earth. That's what I plan to tell the scooter rental place."

Marlee knew it was the wrong thing to do, but she giggled.

Matteo cast her a look and shook his head.

"It's just such a day of firsts," Marlee said. "Scooter ride, donkey train, and now hitchhiking. It feels kind of amazing when you just surrender to what's happening, instead of fighting it. I don't even really care if I make the pedicure or not."

"Surrender," Mackay said brightly. "The place where the adventure begins."

Matteo contemplated that word. *Surrender.* He was riding in the bed of a truck on top of corn husks bundled together. The breeze from the open-air ride made the temperature feel perfect.

The family who owned the truck were crowded into the cab singing, their joy drifting back to him, and Marlee was nestled under his arm, fast asleep, her head on his chest, her breath causing puddles of warmth on his skin. Her scent—lemony—was mingled with the scent of the sun on the corn husks.

He was not sure when, if ever, he had felt so content.

It pressed at the edges of his contentment that

to feel this way was dangerous. It made a person open, vulnerable to being hurt.

Matteo had enjoyed the day.

More than enjoyed it, really. He had been exhilarated by it.

By every second of it, even the loss of the scooter. He had not been this spontaneous for a long time.

If ever.

He had enjoyed Marlee.

No, more. Been exhilarated by her.

She was beautiful. And she was interesting and smart. He wasn't sure if she made him laugh, or if being with her opened him, in some way, to the delights of life that he had been closed off from before.

Whichever, she was just the type of woman who could make a man forget the inherent dangers of caring about someone.

He gave in to the temptation to touch her hair. It would be so easy to care about her.

Deeply.

To take it one step further...

She stirred, and that dress hitched up a few inches further on the shapely length of her leg. He thought of her in the water last night, goddess rising, and snatched his hand away from the sun-warmed silk of her hair.

He needed to get this situation back into control.

His control.

And he needed to do it fast.

The truck lurched to a stop in front of the resort, and Marlee's eyes snapped open. She struggled to sitting, and he noticed the linen pattern of his shirt was traced in the softness of the skin on her cheek.

She took him in, those gorgeous green eyes bewildered. She looked at the bed of corn husks around her. Drowsy confusion gave way to a smile that tickled her lips.

Beautiful lips. Wide and generous.

Lips that begged to be kissed. He remembered the faint taste of them that had lingered on that cigar they had shared a taste of.

She touched his shirt. "Look," she said, her voice husky—and sexy—with sleep. "I drooled on you."

Matteo had a shocking thought of what a life could be like waking up to her.

He leaped up and scrambled off the back of the truck. Unfortunately, chivalry demanded he help her down. He turned back for her.

Marlee had stood and was navigating the corn husks. Her dress was rumpled. There was a smudge—donkey spit?—across the front of it. There was also a corn husk tangled in her hair.

He was not sure a woman had ever looked so beautiful.

He held out his hand to her, and when hers closed around his, it felt right and good.

And terrible and wrong.

And as if that control he longed for could be taken by such a simple thing as her hand in his.

She let go of his hand and put her arms around his neck, instead, and of their own accord his hands closed around her waist and he lifted her down off the truck bed.

There was something about the small gesture that made him feel strong. Masculine. Possessive. Protective.

The chatter of the happy family they had shared the truck with died. So did the street noises: cars, horns, vendors calling, children laughing, chickens cackling.

His whole world felt as if it was this: her cornhusk-tangled hair, her eyes, the plumpness of her bottom lip, the sweet sensation of her body pressed into the length of his.

Surrender.

CHAPTER EIGHT

SURRENDER. MATTEO HAD not said the word out loud, and yet it was as if Marlee had heard it. Her body relaxed against his, and she tilted her head upward, her gaze sleepy, unconsciously sensual.

And then her gaze drifted to his lips. Hungry. Curious.

He knew, when her tongue flicked out and wetted her own lips, what was coming. He commanded himself to go into full retreat. But something stronger within him commanded something else.

Surrender.

Pressed full against him, she stood on her tiptoes and her lips touched his lips.

Her kiss was a study in contradiction: sweet and sexy, sharp and soft, questing and fulfilled.

She tasted of salt and wine and of a bottomless womanly mystery.

Everything in him cried to go deeper, to tangle yet further, to know her more, to explore her secrets.

Thankfully, before he totally lost his mind—forgot they were on a public street and tangled his hands in her hair to pull her closer and claim her lips more thoroughly—she pulled away.

Her blush rose above the sun-kissed glow the day had given her cheeks. She laughed, self-conscious.

"Thank you for an incredible day," she said so sweetly awkward that he wanted to kiss her again.

Surrender.

Was it really where the adventure began?

Or was it where life as you knew it ended?

Matteo realized he did not want to find out. He needed to get a hold of himself. He needed to do it now.

It would be easy, wouldn't it?

Their mission was completed. He didn't have to see her again until the wedding. No, that wasn't quite right. There was the rehearsal dinner tomorrow night. That would give him a time to reconstruct his battered barriers.

"Yes," Matteo said, "It's been an interesting day."

It was a deliberate understatement. His tone was formal, and he could see the bewildered hurt in her eyes. He moved past her before his resolve was slayed by that. He opened the gate to the resort and held it for her.

They walked in silence along the pathway to her cabana where he had first encountered her.

It seemed impossible that that was less than twenty-four hours ago. He already felt as if he knew her, deeply.

Which was the dangerous part. Wasn't it better to hurt her now, than later?

This was what he knew: the more you cared about someone, the deeper the hurt you could cause them.

There was no sense following the intrigue that beckoned to him from those jade green eyes. There was no sense following that trail of laughter they had been on all day. Thinking of her laughter made him look again at her lips.

No, there was no sense following *that* desire any further.

One of them had to be the sensible one. He felt vaguely resentful that it didn't appear it was going to be her.

If you couldn't count on a librarian to be sensible, what exactly could you count on?

"I'll leave it to you to brief Fiona," he suggested.

"Sure," she said, uncertainly.

"And I'll see you at the rehearsal dinner."

"But—I thought we might... I thought we had—" She stopped herself. The injured look gave way to one of pride. She knew he was brushing her off.

She apparently had no appreciation whatso-ever for all the pain he was saving them both.

"Yes," she said, her voice tight and wounded. "That's fine. All right."

"I have to report the stolen scooter," he said, trying a little too late, to soften the blow. "As the only crime that's ever occurred on Coconut Cay, it'll probably be complicated. I don't want to drag you into it. You know, in case it involves jail time."

His attempt to lighten things fell flat, which made him want to try even harder to coax a smile out of her.

"Not that that would bother a hardened out-law such as yourself."

No smile. Marlee gave him a long, level look that let him know she was not fooled, and then, head high and chin up, she turned away from him.

"Plus," he said weakly, knowing the damage was done, "according to the schedule, I'm sup-posed to golf with the guys tomorrow."

"Oh," she said, trying for breeziness and fail-ing, "Of course. The schedule! Golf."

Her tone made him feel like a complete ass.

Which, come to think of it, he was.

Neither of them had noticed Fiona barreling toward them until it was too late and she was standing, hands on hips, right in front of them.

"There you are! You missed the pedicures," Fiona snapped at Marlee, without greeting either of them. "Everything is going wrong. Everything."

Matteo shot Marlee a look and gave her a slight shake of his head letting her know that now didn't seem to be the time to break it to the harried bride she might have to substitute a donkey for the horse in her photos.

"Let me see what color you got," Marlee said soothingly. "I'm sure I can get a pedicure tomorrow, so that we all have matching toes, just like you wanted."

"As a matter of fact, you can't," Fiona said. "She only comes one day a week, so it's a little late to be thinking about what I wanted."

Still, she wiggled a toe at them, and he caught a glimpse of glittery gold.

"I'll figure it out," Marlee promised.

"I hope so," Fiona said petulantly, and then eyed Marlee. "You must have found a horse."

"Um…"

Fiona leaned a little closer to her and sniffed. "You did!" she said, "I can smell horses!"

She brightened. For a moment Matteo could almost see what Mike saw in her. Almost.

"There are a number of good options," Marlee said carefully.

Fiona visibly relaxed, but instead of acting

grateful, she shot Marlee a look. "Good grief! Did you get right in the corral with them? You have something in your hair. And on your dress. You look like you lost a fight with a cat."

So much for glimpsing what Mike saw in her! Her tone was so acid that Matteo felt a need to put his body between Marlee and Fiona.

"You don't," he said firmly to Marlee when he saw she was clearly calculating if that was why he had turned cool toward her.

Fiona glared at him as if she was actually thinking of arguing about it, and then with a miffed sigh turned and left.

He stood there feeling the shock of the encounter.

"Good God," he said. "Is she always like this? She was downright vugly."

"She looked like she'd been crying," Marlee said.

"She did?"

"She just wants everything to be perfect."

He made a note to remember Fiona when he was thinking control was the be-all and end-all of life.

"I'm not sure why you would come to her defense," he said.

"Fiona didn't have the best childhood," Marlee confided in him. "We've known each other since fifth grade. That's when she moved in down the

street from me. Her house was always so chaotic.
I think that's why she's so intent on perfection
with the wedding. From the moment she met
Mike it was as if she felt she could finally have
what she thought everyone else had."

Matteo looked at her and saw yet another side
to Marlee—a deep well of kindness and compassion.

"If getting my toes painted gold will help her
feel better, even a little bit, I'll do it," she said.

And somehow, after seeing how her friend
had treated her, and how she had responded, he
couldn't just abandon her because he needed to
be in control.

Fiona had just managed to shatter his beliefs
about control, anyway.

"Do you want to have dinner together tonight?" he asked her.

He was shocked at himself.

Because ten minutes ago he had promised to
pull back from the temptations of Marlee. And
now, he seemed to be entangling himself further than ever.

She stood stock-still and searched his face.

It occurred to him she was going to say no.

"No," Marlee said, injecting far more firmness
into her tone than she felt. How did anyone say
no to spending more time with him?

It had been one of the best days of her life, sun-kissed and sizzling with connection, fun and adventure.

Of course, then she had to go wreck it all by kissing him. No wonder he was trying to run away from her.

She'd had too much to drink. She'd slobbered on his shirt. She looked—and smelled, according to Fiona—as if she'd been mucking out stalls.

While she'd been thinking *best day ever*, who knew what he had been thinking? He came from a different world, no doubt filled with glamorous novelties that made scooter rides and donkeys and traveling in a truck full of corn husks seem, well, corny to him.

Marlee had known from the outset he was way out of her league, and when he'd dismissed her—said he would see her again at the rehearsal dinner—she had realized he was reminding her of that.

Now he was changing his mind.

She hadn't missed how he had inserted himself protectively between her and Fiona. It had felt rather nice, but on the other hand, she wasn't going to spend more time with him because he felt sorry for her.

The heart that had blossomed at his gesture of protectiveness whined that she could take whatever she could get, even if it was motivated by pity!

Her heart wanted her to let him be in charge: he'd decide when he'd have enough, when they were going to spend time together and when they weren't.

Even though she'd been abjectly disappointed when he'd pulled the plug after their wonderful day, Marlee was so aware something was shifting in her.

You could not have a day like today and not be changed by it, not have a stronger sense of yourself and what you wanted.

She realized she had always felt that with her ex—as if she was begging for his time, for little crumbs of his affection. She realized now she had not required nearly enough. Not of Arthur, who was just Arthur, in the same way Fiona was just Fiona. She had not required enough of herself. She had not set her standards high enough.

Maybe it was the story of her life.

And it was never too late to change that story, so even as a part of her said, *Yes, please, let's have dinner together*, another part of her held proudly firm.

"No," she repeated. "I'm not hungry. I'm eager to wash off the donkey dust. You need to go make your stolen scooter report. Call me if you need bail, otherwise I'll see you at the rehearsal dinner. Enjoy your golf game!"

Matteo looked utterly shocked. Marlee was willing to bet it was the first time he'd ever had a woman call the shots on his charming self. Particularly refusing his invitation in preference to washing off donkey dust!

As she turned away, went into the cabana and shut the door on his stunned face, Marlee found herself smiling.

She was *glad* she had kissed him. Shaken him out of his stuffy world enough to make him take a startled step back from her.

It felt good to take her power back, even if there was a price to pay. And so when the temptation was to retreat from all her discoveries—stay in her room with a book that evening—she didn't. Using the very rudimentary seamstress kit she always traveled with—librarians ferreted out every potential disaster, after all—she took the bra she had worn last night off the shower bar where she had flung it after its return this morning and sewed the breakaway clasp firmly and permanently shut. She wouldn't be needing that feature anytime soon.

Then she stripped, exchanged the bra she was wearing for the repaired one and slipped a swim cover-up on. She then went to the resort store and bought some chicken being kept warm under a burner.

Then, she took the pathway past her cabana. The cigar was still sitting on the wall where he had left it last night and she picked it up.

Because it was litter, not because he had tasted it!

Then she went down to the beach she had shared with Matteo.

She watched the sun go down in a brief but glorious display of color. For one suspended moment, the ocean turned to fire and every grain of sand on the beach glittered gold.

It was, she told herself firmly, the perfect ending to the best day ever. She didn't need a man to make it all lovelier. It couldn't be any lovelier than it already was.

But then, just as she was on the brink of convincing herself that was true, a shiver up and down her spine let her know she was no longer alone on the beach.

She turned her head to see Matteo coming across the sand. She switched her attention quickly back to the orb of the sun, disappearing on the horizon as if it was plunging into the sea. For a woman discovering her own power, the mere sight of him coming toward her in the soft golden light was doing things to her heartbeat. She felt weak instead of strong.

"Hey," he said, quietly. "Beautiful night."

"It is," she agreed. "Probably looks even better after your close brush with jail time."

The question was, what was he doing here after his close brush with her lips?

"I don't think there is a jail. I reported the missing scooter at the rental place. Same response as Mackay. *No, no, not stolen. Borrowed.* They seemed to have every confidence it will just show up."

"So what brings you here? Extra time now that you've been freed of potential legal wrangling?"

I couldn't get your ravishing kiss out of my mind. Ha ha.

"Fiona saw me. She told me to find you and give you this." He dropped a tiny brown bag on her lap. "When you weren't at your place, I thought you might be here."

So he hadn't sought her out of his own accord. It was an *errand.* He was here because he had been *instructed.*

He was probably thinking, *Pathetic thing. Reliving memories of last night and very ordinary, workaday kisses that she thought were ravishing.*

Reminder: girls like her were not even on the radar of men like him.

Marlee told herself sternly that she was rethinking the kind of girl she was. Her hand found the cigar she had picked up, and she clamped it between her lips.

"Those are habit-forming," he warned her mildly.

"Only if you light them." *Or taste another person's lips on them.*

He nodded solemnly. "An outlaw prop."

Without invitation he dropped down in the sand beside her.

"I thought you said you weren't hungry," he said, eyeing the chicken.

Good. He understood her refusal had been about him, not about hunger. She shrugged.

"How is it?"

"After Mackay's mother's? Barely edible." She took the unlit cigar from her lips and held it between her fingers, as if she intended to light it at any time.

CHAPTER NINE

"CAN I HAVE A PIECE?"

Matteo's errand was done. Why was he hanging around? Marlee thought.

"Have a piece of chicken at your own risk. But don't feel you have to sit in the sand with me. You've achieved your mission."

She put down the cigar—who was she kidding? She was no outlaw. He was right. It was just a prop. She had no hope—ever—of being the real thing. She dug in the bag he had dropped on her lap and drew out the items one by one.

Sheesh. It was pedicure in a bag. The last item she took out was a bottle of glittering gold nail polish.

"See? Matteo, you've saved the world. Or at least the wedding. Donkey acquisition and pedicure rescue all in one day. You must be exhausted. It will probably affect your golf game. That's a shame."

"You're being sarcastic," he said, his voice low. "I've hurt your feelings."

Marlee did not want to be that transparent!

"Is this part of your intention to be more sensitive? It's completely unnecessary. You haven't hurt my feelings."

Matteo regarded her intently. He said nothing. It felt as if he saw straight through her—right to her soul. It was very discomforting.

"I get it. Entirely. You move in different circles than me. No sense the plain-Jane librarian from Seattle getting romantic notions. Not that I was. But I don't blame you for thinking I was. I mean, who wouldn't? I kissed you. It was an impulse. A bad one. But you're pretty easy on the eyes. You have a jet. You're kind of funny and entertaining. But just for your information, I've had a recent breakup. The last thing I'm looking for—"

He cut off the flow of words—good grief, she was babbling—by laying a gentle finger against her lips.

After all she had just said, how could she possibly be having a temptation to nibble that finger?

She should want to bite it! It was insulting. He was silencing her.

"You thought I didn't want to see you until the rehearsal dinner because I found you a—what did you say—plain Jane? You think I found you unattractive?"

His voice was a low growl that felt like a touch shivering along her spine.

She nodded, which had the unfortunate effect of moving her lips on his finger, creating a sensational feeling.

"Marlee," Matteo said, his voice low and pained, those color-of-the-sea eyes intent on her face, "the exact opposite is true."

She tried to let that sink in, but she couldn't comprehend what he was saying.

"What do you mean," she asked, "the exact opposite is true?"

Matteo looked suddenly uncomfortable.

"It might all be a moot point, anyway," he said. "I don't know if there's going to be a rehearsal dinner."

"What?"

"The lovely bride-to-be is up there throwing a fit at Mike right now."

"About what?"

"Who knows? Gardenias. A delayed champagne delivery. The flower girl's hair. Maybe she wanted Mike to get a pedicure for barefoot pictures in the sand and he missed his appointment. Just like you."

"You're making her sound very unreasonable."

Matteo cast Marlee a look but didn't say anything.

"Okay, she's being a bit of a bridezilla."

"A bit?"

"After what she grew up with, Fiona just

wants it all to be so perfect. That's why she has to have control."

"What did she grow up with?"

Marlee felt as if she had to make a choice. On one hand, she didn't want to reveal personal information about her friend. On the other hand, she didn't want Matteo to think Fiona was purely horrible, with no redeeming characteristics.

"Her mom and dad both drank too much. Her house was crazy. Nothing—and I mean nothing—was predictable, except for the fighting and chaos. I think part of the destination wedding decision was because her mom's terrified of flying. Fiona didn't want them here for her big day. She knew they'd wreck everything."

Matteo was silent. "Thank you for telling me that. It puts things in a different light. She's very lucky to have you for a friend. Actually, anyone would be lucky to have you for a friend."

There was something about the look in his eyes that a woman could fall toward. But Marlee was pretty sure there was a not-so-subtle message in there.

That maybe they could be *friends*.

Friends didn't kiss each other at the end of the day!

She looked at the bottle of nail polish. "I'm going to put it on and go show her. Maybe it'll be a distraction for her. A 'See? Everything is going to be fine' moment."

His lips twitched.

"It's a lot to ask of toenail polish."

"I don't know. It's an interesting color. It looks like it's been mixed with dreams and fairy dust."

He pretended to inspect the bottle. "A little magic mixed in there."

"Here's to magic," she said, and kicked off her sandals and regarded her toes.

"You don't know any more about nail polish than you do about cigars, do you?"

"And you do?"

"Older sisters," he said. "You don't put it on surrounded by sand. I know that much."

"Oh," she said. "Of course!"

"And if you wanted to swim, we should do that first."

We.

"Because I don't think you can get your toes wet for a while after you've painted them."

She noticed the stars winked on in an inky dark sky.

She noticed the air smelled of the sea.

She noticed her breath inside her chest, its simple rise and fall feeling like a celebration of life.

In all its glory, and all its surprises.

You think I don't find you attractive? The exact opposite is true.

It was as good as hearing he'd been dazzled by her kiss.

Still, Matteo was giving her mixed messages. He wanted to be just friends? Or he wanted more?

Maybe it was time for her to make some choices!

And her choice, right now, was just to embrace the moment.

She stood up, peeled off the swimsuit cover-up and let it drift to the sand beside her. She stood there before him in her underwear again, feeling bold.

He had never clarified exactly what he meant by *the exact opposite is true* but Marlee could see the obvious truth in his eyes.

He found her beautiful.

It allowed her to do what she had never done— to see herself as beautiful, too. She liked the way his eyes had darkened to midnight as he took in her moon-painted body.

"You're going to try that, um outfit, again?" he asked, his voice hoarse. "You do like to live dangerously."

"Only recently. Allowing my inner outlaw free rein. I fixed it, anyway. No wardrobe malfunctions tonight."

"More the shame, that," he said.

And then he rose to his feet, and with a shout of laughter, chased her into the water.

Finally, exhausted from playing in the ocean like children, they went and threw themselves on her blanket on the sand. She shivered.

"We should go in," he said. "It's warm here, but it's still chilly at night if you're wet."

We?

What did that mean? She should offer him a nightcap?

"We still have to paint your toenails."

This time she said it out loud, with a lifted eyebrow. *"We?"* She didn't actually think it would be safe to let him touch her feet.

"I know lots about pedicures."

She remembered his lips on her toes last night and shivered.

"I told you, I have sisters."

That took some of the white heat out of her mental meanderings.

"Time to go," he said, getting up. "You're freezing."

Actually, she felt as if she was melting. He waited for her to gather up her things, then shook the sand out of her blanket and put it over her shoulders.

It was a small gesture. It felt so nice.

Inside her cabana, he shooed her into the shower. She debated what to bring in there to change into.

What exactly did one wear when the world's most gorgeous man had offered to help with your pedicure?

She wanted it to be super sexy without giving the appearance she was trying to be sexy. Finally, she chose an oversize pajama top that came to her midthigh. She usually would have worn the top with pajama bottoms. Tonight, she left those off.

She looked at herself in the full-length mirror before she went out into the main room. Her hair was damp and curling. Her face glowed from her day out in the sun. Her eyes were luminous. She had what some might have called a come-hither look.

She wondered what she was playing at. What were *they* playing at? How was this all going to unfold?

That, she told herself firmly, was the librarian talking.

That was not how outlaws talked to themselves at all! A proper outlaw didn't think of consequences, or the future.

A proper outlaw embraced the dangerous thrills of the moment.

She went out into the main room. Matteo

glanced up at her, then looked quickly back at his phone.

His phone, she thought, disappointed about her wasted come-hither look. Arthur had always seemed to find his phone more interesting than her, too.

"You caught me," Matteo said, and flashed the phone at her.

She burst out laughing.

The screen read: *How to do a pedicure like a pro.*

"You said you'd done this with your sisters."

"Well, a hundred years ago."

"You look much younger than you are," she said, giving him a wide-eyed look. "How many sisters?"

"Two. Mia and Emma."

"Are you close?"

"Oh, yeah. We run the family business together. I also have two nieces and two nephews. They're incorrigible brats."

"You adore them."

His easy grin gave her the answer.

She liked it that he was close to his sisters and his family.

"Okay, enough chitchat," he said sternly. "Come over here and sit down."

She went and sat at the sofa, while he sat on a stool facing it. Really? A pinch-me moment.

The most gorgeous man in the world was at her feet.

"This is serious business," he told her, so seriously that she wanted to laugh. "I don't want to be distracted and chop off your toe. A large, bandaged appendage would wreck the wedding pictures."

"I don't think you could chop off my toe with those," she said, pointing at the clippers. Then she frowned. "You don't think you're going to use those, do you?"

"It's step four: trim and shape toenails."

He took her foot. His hand slid along it as he eyed her toenails. Considering he was only touching her foot, Marlee felt ripples through every cell of her body!

"Just put the nail polish on!"

"Uh-uh. I'm a follow-the-instructions kind of guy."

He did something with his fingertips to her instep that she was pretty sure was not in the instructions.

"That's a long way from my toes," she said, through gritted teeth.

"I know," he said and tilted his head to smile at her.

Marlee wondered how she was going to survive this.

CHAPTER TEN

MATTEO LET HIS hand slide along her instep one more time. Then, with a let's-get-to-work sigh, he picked up the toenail clippers that had come in the kit.

"Give me those," Marlee said. "You are *not* cutting my toenails."

"Wait!" He held them out of her reach when she grabbed for them. "I missed steps. We're nowhere near the part where we argue about toenail cutting."

"Humph."

"Step one," he read, his officiousness coaxing an inward smile out of her, if not an outward one. "Soak your toes and feet. Have you got a basin I can fill?"

"I think the shower and ocean probably looked after that."

"Okay, moving along, then. Step two: get rid of any dead skin."

"That's gross. Let's just skip to the painting the nails part."

"Then we're at step three: remove old polish."

"There is none," she snapped. At this moment,

she *hated* it that there was none. It made her feel unglamorous and downright dull.

He had already moved on. "Step four: trimming and shaping your toenails. Now we're at the arguing part."

"They are fine the way they are," Marlee insisted.

He gave her a look, took her foot firmly and inspected it. He was probably deciding they were librarian toenails, nothing elegant about them at all.

"I cut them straight across the top like that because it's recommended to prevent ingrown toenails."

Who said that to a man like him? Sheesh! Worst conversation ever. Still, she shivered at the way her feet looked in his hands, pale against his darker flesh, delicate against his obvious strength.

"Are you still cold?" Matteo asked, glancing up at her.

"No, you're tickling me."

"Oh," he said, pleased. "Ticklish feet. I'll file that away for future reference."

Future?

There was no future, that was what she had to remember about him. They had been thrown together for a few days. After the wedding they would never see each other again.

Which should have given her pause about what was happening between them right now, some exciting and dangerous awareness sizzling in the air between them.

But Marlee was already not who she had been twenty-four hours ago.

Because instead of the fact she would never see him again giving her pause, it felt as if it was giving her license.

Still holding her instep, he studied her toes intently. He leaned very close to them. She could feel his breath tickling them. If he kissed them, as he had done last night, she was pretty sure any hope of a friendship would be lost, and she was going to exercise the liberty that came with never seeing him again.

His mouth on her toes would unleash something in her. She would not be responsible for what happened next. It felt as if a secret side of her was crying to get out, and that side was totally uninhibited.

Shockingly wild. Unabashedly sexy.

He did not kiss her toes, and Marlee was not at all sure if she was disappointed or relieved.

She was aware, too, that she was quite literally leaving it all in his hands.

"I think you're right," he decided. "They're already pretty short. No trim required."

She did something she would not have done

twenty-four hours ago. She reached out and touched the silk of his hair with her fingertips.

"What did you mean when you said the exact opposite was true?" she asked him.

Matteo felt her hand in his hair. He glanced up at Marlee.

He was aware he had placed himself in this position, even knowing the dangers inherent to it.

For him, it was delightful that she had no idea how beautiful she was.

In the short time he had known her, he already knew that her beauty not just on the outside of her, but on the inside of her, too.

He had to fight the temptations of her. And he had to let her know why, even if it meant doing what he least liked to do.

Exposing his own fears and insecurities.

It felt as though if ever there was a person he could trust with his deepest secrets, it was her. How could he feel that way?

He barely knew her.

On the other hand, you couldn't spend a day with someone like Marlee and not feel as if you knew her.

He had seen her laugh and fall in love with donkeys and embrace adventures and roll with the punches.

But it was her gentle compassion toward a friend who might not have deserved it that made Matteo feel, not just as if he knew her, but as if he knew her deeply.

To her heart. To her soul.

His trust in her felt extraordinary.

He focused on the array of items that had come from the pedicure kit. Her hand was still tickling his hair.

"Step five," he said, avoiding her question about what he'd really meant, "toe separators. Never mind that we missed the first four steps."

She laughed, low in her throat. It was a sound that could make a man forget he had a history that warned him away from women like this one.

Gently, he inserted the toe separators. Her hand went very still in his hair.

"Step six: base coat." He waggled the bottle at her. "Crucial, apparently."

Carefully, he took out the brush and began to apply a thin layer of the base coat. He began to speak, knowing he had to warn her off, now, before it was too late.

"My mother and my father had a grand passion for each other," Matteo said. He could hear the roughness of pain in the slight hoarseness of his own voice.

"They could not be together enough. They

could not keep their hands off each other. The romance never died—the little gifts, the love notes, the exchanged looks, the heat between them. We didn't have a family so much as the two of them, my mother and father, being the sun, and the rest of us orbiting around their light."

He finished the toes of her right foot and moved on to the left. There was a stillness in the room that reminded him of a cathedral.

"And then my mother got sick," Matteo said. "And then she got sicker. And then she died. My father, this man who had been so powerful, and so in control of everything, except his love for her, could not change it. When she died, she took part of his soul with her."

He swallowed hard, capped the base coat, and blew on her toes to dry them. He opened the bottle of gold.

"He never got it back."

Matteo stared at Marlee's toes. Were they blurry? No, of course not! He was a man in control of his emotions.

If she had said anything, he was not sure he could have continued. He dared not look at her. If he saw softness in her eyes, he felt as if it would finish everything he believed about his own strength.

He dabbed the gold onto her nails, took a deep

breath and finished what he had to say just as he put the last stroke of the polish on.

"His grief ignored the fact he had children to live for, and it almost destroyed a business that had been in our family four hundred years."

Finally, Matteo got to *the* question.

"I didn't say I didn't want to see you again until the dinner because I don't find you attractive, Marlee. Maybe you see yourself as a plain-Jane librarian, but I don't. I feel something. Don't you?"

Marlee didn't say anything, and he didn't dare look at her for her answer.

"I feel it," he continued, his voice a ragged whisper, "shivering in the air between us. A terrifying potential. I'm not sure I'm brave enough to know what you could be to me."

He set down her feet abruptly. He looked everywhere but at her.

"I feel foolish saying that." He glanced at his watch. "I've known you all of twenty-four hours. But that's what I wanted you to know. That the exact opposite is true. You may be the most beautiful woman I have ever encountered."

And then finally, Matteo looked at her.

He saw the stillness he had experienced in the room reflected in her face. The greenness of her eyes reminded him of a cool pond on a hot day, a place a man could dive into and find relief from everything that troubled him.

Did he throw himself into such a promise of sanctuary as Marlee offered, or did he flee from it?

What was in the air between them felt as impossible to fight as a tsunami would be if it swept up that beach.

"I've burdened you with my difficulties," he said, and heard the stiffness in his voice. "I'm sorry. I don't usually have jet lag, but I may be suffering from it now. It has—"

Weakened me. Made me less a man.

"—been extraordinarily inappropriate."

With what small remnants of his strength that remained, Matteo made the decision to find higher ground. Without another word, he carefully lined up the things left over from the pedicure kit, got to his feet and walked out of the cabana.

Wiggling her freshly painted toes, Marlee sat there, stunned by the abruptness of Matteo's departure. She felt abandoned. And let down.

Who told someone they might be the most beautiful woman they had ever encountered and then forsook them?

Confusingly, the sting of desertion warred with the incredible gift of Matteo's trust.

"Which he is now sorry he bestowed," she reminded herself sternly. "Jet lag–inspired confidences!"

Besides, she shared his terror of the forces that were drawing them together, didn't she? Though there were much larger forces drawing them apart if she thought about it. Their fears and past experiences formed quite a wedge.

And so did time.

The wedding was on Saturday. She had to see him at the rehearsal dinner tomorrow night, and at the wedding, of course. She could avoid encounters of the truly scary kind. That was what he wanted to do. He was being very sensible.

It would be dumb to put her already battered heart at risk! Matteo had exited in the nick of time, and she would respect that.

The decision for self-preservation made, Marlee got up and, mindful of the fragility of freshly painted nails, tiptoed cautiously into the bathroom. She used the hair dryer to finish drying her toes, then glanced at the clock. It was late, but chances of her going to sleep were nil.

Her family had always taught her the remedy for discomfort was to stop thinking about yourself and do something for someone in need.

Marlee thought that Fiona might be up and in need of comfort. That was why she had done her toenails in the first place, she reminded herself.

She changed out of her pajamas and into that horrible but exceedingly comfy pink sweat suit, then made her way across the darkened resort to Fiona's suite.

As she had suspected, the light was on inside. She knocked lightly on the door. After a long pause, Fiona flung it open.

Her face fell when she saw it was Marlee.

"I hoped you were Mike," she said, glancing over Marlee's shoulder as if she might have hidden Mike somewhere behind her.

"I just came to show you my toenails," Marlee said, hoping to lighten Fiona's mood. She lifted one leg and wiggled her toes.

Fiona bent over and looked at them. "Oh," she said, with an exasperated sigh of long-suffering. "Didn't you get my text?"

Marlee put her leg down. "What?"

"I sent you a picture of what I wanted. I'll show you."

Fiona went and grabbed her phone. "It was bridesmaid photo of the year."

Marlee looked at the picture. Four perfect feet were photographed against a backdrop of powdered sugar sand. Each one's toenails were painted gold, but each had a tiny white flower on it.

"You're supposed to have the flower on your

fourth toe. I have one on my big toe, Kathy has one on her second toe, Brenda on her third."

"Well, I'll just have to be plain gold," Marlee said, stung by the criticism.

"You're wrecking everything," Fiona said.

"*I'm* wrecking everything?"

Marlee contemplated catching the next flight home. Three birds with one stone: she wouldn't have to steel herself against meeting Matteo again; she wouldn't have to put up with Fiona; and she wouldn't have to *really* wreck everything by admitting she'd found a donkey instead of a horse.

"I could tell by your face you hate the dress I picked for you. You missed the welcome party by the pool. You missed the pedicures. You're acting like you hate it all."

And here she thought she had been hiding that so well! Marlee was very aware that there was something about having spent the day with Matteo that had brought out this more forthright side of her. She took a deep breath.

"Fiona, I have gone to a great deal of trouble, time and expense to be here for you. I spent the whole day trying to find you, um, an equine. I did miss the pool get-together, and I wasn't here for the spa thing, but I've done my best to give you what you wanted. And instead of being grateful, instead of acting as if you want me here, you're just being self-centered and mean."

How much of having a man at her feet admitting he thought she was beautiful and that he found himself terribly attracted to her had given her the courage to say this?

Fiona's mouth fell open.

"And I *do* hate the dress," Marlee said, while she was getting things off her chest and being courageous. "I'm not wearing it."

"Well, you won't have to," Fiona said, and burst into tears, "because there is not going to be a wedding!"

Marlee took her friend by the elbow and guided her to the couch.

"What's going on, Fiona?" She sank onto the couch beside her.

"Mike said the same things to me as you. Only he wasn't as nice about it. He called me the B-word."

"I'm sorry," Marlee said, and she genuinely was.

"The B-word! My dad used to call my mom that when they were fighting. I screamed at Mike that I wouldn't marry him now if he was the last man on earth.

"How can this be happening to me?" she whimpered. "I knew my parents wouldn't come if I had it here, but it doesn't matter. It's the very same as if they were here. Fighting. Chaos. Name-calling… Marlee, I'm going to end up just like you," she whispered as if that was the worst thing on earth. "Abandoned at the altar."

Marlee considered that for a moment, and the truth unfolded in her like a flag unfurling.

"It was the best thing that ever happened to me."

CHAPTER ELEVEN

It was the best thing that ever happened to me.

"What?" Fiona said. "You're devastated! You've looked sad for six months."

Either Fiona was actually capable of seeing how others felt, or she was worried about *that* look for the photos. Marlee decided to give her the benefit of the doubt.

"I was sad. But I'm not now."

Marlee could probably pinpoint just about the precise moment when that had happened, and it had been when she had embraced a bolder side, and been drinking rum and contemplating smoking a cigar. The moment when she had met the man who would change it all.

It was as if from that point a new world had opened to her. A world full of wonder.

"You and Arthur were so perfect for each other," Fiona said dejectedly. "When it didn't work, it kind of shook my sense of safety. It made me aware that anything could happen to anybody at any time."

"Why do you say we were perfect for each other?"

"You were just so *stable*. That's what made the breakup so shocking. You were like your mom and dad."

Marlee smiled. "Yes, we were. Arthur actually brought that up when he called it off. He said we were much too young to be so settled. He used the word *comfy*."

"Like your mom and dad! That's what I've yearned for my whole life."

"He said we were like two worn recliners in front of the TV set."

Fiona giggled through her tears. "Okay. Maybe that's a little *too* comfy."

"If I had married him," Marlee said softly, arriving at the realization herself for the first time, "I would have missed so much. Boldness. Adventure. Spontaneity."

"Oh! As if *you* are going to embrace those things now!"

"I might surprise you," Marlee said.

"I'm sorry. I didn't mean that to sound as if you're dull and boring. It's just, I rely on you to be the stable one." Fiona sighed. "I've been totally awful, haven't I?"

"Look, I get it. I know what you come from."

"You're the only one here who actually knows. I mean, I've told Mike I didn't have the best family life, and he's seen it for himself when he's met my parents, but I've always controlled everything about him meeting them. Dinner in a nice restaurant with strict timelines. Like, I'd book a show right after, so that they didn't have time to…well, you know, do what they do.

"I've never even had him to their house. It's such an embarrassment to me. Who knows what you'd find this week? A window somebody has thrown something through? A wrecked car in the yard? I wanted this whole wedding to be like the opposite of that. I wanted it to be classy and romantic and beautiful."

"As if you were leaving all that behind."

"Exactly," Fiona said sadly.

"Fiona, you can't leave parts of yourself behind. Believe it or not, some of the things that are best about you come from that."

She contemplated that for a moment. "You think so?"

"You need to go talk to Mike and tell him exactly what you told me just now. You need to let him know why being in control is so important to you. And you need to let him know you believe in the power of love, above all else."

Fiona looked at her hopefully, through wet eyes. "Okay," she said. "Am I a total mess?"

"You are."

"I need to—"

"You need to go to him exactly as you are, Fiona. Exactly."

Fiona stared at her.

"No makeup?" she whispered. "He's never seen me without makeup."

"You wear your makeup to bed?" Marlee asked, astonished.

"Just a little bit."

"Doesn't it end up on the pillowcase?"

"I look horrible without any makeup on."

"I'm sure he doesn't love you because of your makeup."

"I'm not even sure he does love me."

"Go find out. Be brave. Fiona—" she said the next part carefully "—think about what *he* needs. Not what you need."

"Okay," Fiona finally said, as if she was a child who had been given a reprehensible task to fulfill.

Marlee made her way back to her own cabana. She thought she might lie awake for a while but found she was pleasantly exhausted from her day of sunshine and unexpected adventure. She fell asleep thinking about those words.

Be brave.

When her cell phone rang beside her bed, she glanced at her bedside clock. It was one in the morning. She had the crazy hope it was Matteo, even though they had never had a reason to exchange phone numbers.

But it wasn't. It was Fiona.

"The wedding is on!" she cried.

"That's great," Marlee said, sleepy but genuinely happy for her friend.

"Mike hadn't seen me without makeup before and he said I looked *adorbs.*"

"That's true love," Marlee said.

"Isn't it? And my face was all blotchy and tear-stained and he didn't even care."

"That guy is a gem. I've always thought so."

"He thinks the same of you. You were part of what we fought about."

"Me?"

"I was, er, complaining about you missing the warm-up party at the pool and the pedicure, and he said I was being insensitive. He said maybe all this wedding stuff made you sad."

Marlee contemplated that. It made her uncomfortable that she was being talked about, especially in the context of Mike pitying her.

"He seemed very relieved when I told him just now that you decided your wedding cancellation was a good thing. He never liked Arthur for you. He didn't think you should just go for the first guy who paid attention to you."

Again, Marlee did not like the sensation of being talked about, her life and choices dissected. She didn't like it at all that she was seen as some kind of fading wallflower, so pleased at any kind of male attention that her marriage had been seen as an act of desperation instead of love. How much of that was true? She was silent.

"Now that we're on," Fiona said, moving right along, "do you think you could do something about that flower?"

She was confused since she had just been thinking of wallflowers. "What? What flower?"

"The white flower on the fourth toe."

"Um—" Marlee suddenly wasn't sure Fiona had learned anything at all from her wedding nearly not happening.

"I'm not sure painting a white flower on my toe is in my skill set." She was pretty sure it was not in Matteo's, either. Not that she planned to ask him!

"I know you'll figure it out," Fiona said cheerfully. "Thank you for being there for me tonight. Best friend ever!"

And then the phone went dead.

That left Marlee to lie awake, thinking about people pitying her. But her thoughts soon drifted to contemplation of Matteo's abrupt departure last night. She understood why he had gone. He was terrified of love.

He'd made that clear. He had watched it destroy his father, and he was, understandably, steering away from it.

Lying in the darkness of her room, Marlee thought about the words she had said to Fiona.

Think about what he needs.

She had meant it in the context of Mike, but she found herself thinking about Matteo. He appeared to be the man who had everything, and yet he had revealed a damaged heart to her.

It struck her as sad that a man who had accomplished so much materially had condemned himself to such a lonely existence.

Really, what he had confided in her was that he wasn't going to care about anyone, because caring hurt too much.

Of course he had his sisters, his nieces and nephews, but she wondered how much he held back, even from them.

"You can't fix this," she whispered to herself.

But suddenly she was ashamed that she had made the decision to avoid Matteo, to follow his lead, for self-preservation.

That was not the set of values she had grown up with. Maybe it was even the kind of safe decision that inspired pity for her from people like Mike.

It was two more days.

They didn't have to fall in love.

She shivered as that thought entered her mind.

They just had to believe it was okay to care about each other. It was okay to let their guard down. It was okay to have fun and believe that life had natural checks and balances.

It held sorrow and joy.

It was okay to be curious and open to what happened next. Why not ask him to expand his skill set a little bit?

The next morning, in the safest place on earth, Marlee had absolutely no problem getting his room number out of the front desk clerk. She probably could have gotten the key if she'd asked for it!

Her heart beating unreasonably, she found her way to his room.

Except it wasn't exactly a room. Matteo's villa made her tiny cabana look like a shoebox. She suddenly didn't feel at all as confident that she knew what anybody needed. She had deliberately dressed casually—shorts, sandals, a white shirt—but now she wished she'd given in to the temptation to buy a second sundress from the resort boutique.

Too late for doubts! She took a deep breath.

She knocked on the door. Again, Marlee gave herself the same advice she'd given Fiona.

Be brave.

Think about what he needed, not what she needed.

The door swung open and Matteo stood there.

A towel was wrapped around his waist.

She totally forgot about what he needed, or what she needed.

"Do you open your door like that in Switzerland?" she croaked.

"Like what?"

"With no clothes on."

He glanced down at himself. He looked at her, and a small smile tickled his lips at her discomfort.

"You've seen me in my swim shorts," he said. "I don't think this is any less modest."

"Um…"

"Unless," he said wickedly, "there was a wardrobe malfunction."

She gulped.

He laughed. "What gives me the pleasure this morning?"

A reminder that last night he had been *sorry* about the confidences he had shared with her, sorry he had shown her his poor, bruised heart.

It came back to her why she was here.

To rescue him, the man who had everything, from his self-imposed prison of loneliness.

She waved a bottle of white nail polish at him. "Fiona wants some modification to the design. Can I come in? I have a picture."

He hesitated, and then with a slight bow, he held the door open to her.

Surrender.

Marlee stepped by him and his shower-fresh scent tickled her nostrils. She was aware of the perfect, deep carve of his chest and how utterly and beautifully masculine he was. She remembered the accidental touches of her fingers on his naked skin when they had swum together.

They were alone in his villa. The potential for danger—of the most delicious kind—seemed high.

But then she came to a full stop. Her mouth fell open as her eyes adjusted from the bright light outside to the dimmer interior of the villa.

The ceilings soared. The couches were white leather. If she sat on one in her white shirt, she would disappear!

The rest of the furniture was rich, subdued and sophisticated. The huge abstract art pieces were gorgeous. The rugs were, no doubt, priceless. A bouquet of island-bright fresh flowers was in a huge vase in the center of a coffee table.

In her cabana, she had gotten a free cigar and a travel-size bottle of rum. The rich and famous got baby-elephant-size bouquets of flowers.

A whole wall was covered in windows that looked out to a pool. A waterfall cascaded off one end of it. Its marble decks were scattered with huge wicker furniture baskets—giant eggs—with bright pillows inside them. Concrete pots held flowering trees and shrubs. There was a bar at the opposite end of the pool from the waterfall.

"Is that a pool?" she asked, though it was obvious it was.

"Yes."

"Just for this unit?" Marlee was aware her voice was slightly strangled.

Matteo wagged a wicked eyebrow at her. "Privacy has its perks."

She glanced down at the towel and blushed. She had assumed he was in the shower, but maybe he'd been in the pool.

In his altogether!

"Why were you going to the ocean to swim that night if you had this at your disposal?" Including, of course, all that privacy!

The danger she had felt a moment ago felt as if it was diluting, like pouring a glass of red wine into the ocean. He was from a different world than her.

A faster world. A more sophisticated world.

He swam in the nude!

Still, now was not the time to lose courage. She had made it past the first barrier, the front door. The second, if she included him being dressed only in a towel, which a few days ago would have been enough to make her turn tail and run.

"It's a palace," she said. *Who did she think she*

was? He was not only from a different world, he was also one of the richest men in that world.

The third barrier appeared to be her own sense of inadequacy, and she was not so certain she could overcome that one.

She had convinced herself he needed rescuing.

It was laughable.

Was it just an excuse to give in to her desire to be with him? There it was—just sharing the same space with him, she became so aware of a deep and all-consuming hunger.

To know him.

To share air with him.

To make him laugh.

To touch him.

To be touched by him.

"What's wrong?" Matteo said, frowning at her.

Marlee reminded herself firmly of the life she had almost had. As comfortable as two old recliners in front of the television set.

She remembered suddenly a part she had not shared with Fiona.

Rump-sprung.

Arthur had called the recliners that he thought represented their future together rump-sprung.

If she wanted a rump-sprung life, she could leave right now. Holding that thought firm, Marlee held her ground.

CHAPTER TWELVE

MATTEO WATCHED MARLEE take in her surroundings. She looked as if she was contemplating bolting.

"Is something wrong?" he asked her, again.

But then she relaxed, and he knew she would stay. He felt inordinately pleased.

He thought about her question. With a pool at his disposal, why had he gone to the ocean to swim that night?

He was not a whimsical man. Not even a little bit.

And yet, it felt as if destiny had drawn him to the ocean, to his path crossing hers, literally.

Last night, after he had opened his heart to her, he had made a decision. No more being weak when he wanted to be strong.

And yet, when he had opened the door to her standing there, clutching that silly bottle of nail polish, something in him had sighed.

With welcome.

And maybe the most dangerous thing of all, hope.

"Nothing's wrong, exactly," she said, looking

about, "but it's all just very glamourous, like the set of a movie."

"Is it?" He looked around, seeing it through her eyes. To him it looked just like a thousand other high-end hotel rooms he had stayed in.

"You don't even know it's out of the ordinary, do you? I mean the bathroom is probably bigger than my whole apartment in Seattle."

"It's not like it's mine," he pointed out.

She didn't look convinced. Her insecurity had a funny effect on him. He wanted to be the one who made her feel secure.

"It's just a rental. I call this decor style 'generic posh.' I mean, look at that painting over there. Would anybody actually hang it in their house?"

"Nobody has a twelve-foot wall in their house!"

"Besides how huge it is, it has no meaning. Big black looping lines."

She cocked her head thoughtfully at it, and he saw, pleased, just a tiny bit of the tension leave her.

"Maybe it's like an inkblot test," she suggested.

"What do you see in it?"

"The LA freeway," she decided, and they both laughed, and Matteo was grateful something eased even further in her. "What about you?"

"Tangled yarn," he decided. "My grandmother used to knit."

He turned back to her and caught a look on her face. Unless he missed his guess, she also knitted. It endeared her to him, and the fact she was embarrassed about it endeared her more.

"I was just having coffee by the pool," he said. "Come join me, and then we'll discuss the latest in bridal demands. Let me guess. It has something to do with photos."

He was satisfied when he coaxed a little laugh from Marlee. "How did you know?"

He lifted a shoulder and led her through to the patio. He settled her at the table and went and got another cup. He poured her a coffee from the carafe on the table, then sank into his chair across from her. She helped herself to cream and sugar and took a sip.

"So good," she said.

The quality of light on Coconut Cay was magnificent. It danced in her hair and lit her eyes.

She was wearing a crisp white shirt today, button-down. She had on a pair of khaki shorts with it.

So good.

How was she making the quintessential tourist outfit look so sexy?

"Are you, um, going to put on some pants?"

"Am I making you uncomfortable?"

"Yes!"

He grinned. "Good."

He deliberately stretched out his legs. She glanced at the length of them, gave him a warning look, then took out her phone and showed him the picture.

"You're kidding, right?" he asked, contemplating the feet in the picture with the tiny flowers painted on the toenails.

"No, I'm afraid not."

"There are people who specialize in painting miniatures. I'm not one of them."

"But you'll try, at least?"

He looked at the picture again. Dangerous to get into this! To be touching her feet, again, the way he had been last night.

When all his barriers had come tumbling down!

So no one was more shocked than he was, to hear himself saying, "Oh, why not? How difficult could it be?"

Actually, it was quite difficult. After they had finished their coffee, Matteo got Marlee settled among the bright, deep cushions of one of those big, egg-shaped wicker things around the pool.

He took her foot in his hand and bent over it, fighting a ridiculous impulse to kiss her instep. Carefully, tongue between his teeth, he took the brush out of the bottle.

"Is your house in Switzerland as palatial as

this?" she asked him. "The house of a man who flies around in his own jet?"

"Do you want to know a secret about me?"

Now he was going to tell her *more* secrets? She leaned up from where she was reclining among the pillows and it weakened him in some delightful way that she *did* want to know a secret about him.

It was just to make her comfortable, he told himself.

"I still live in the same room I had as a boy. To be honest, not much has changed about it. The model airplane my father and I made together still hangs from a fishing line in one corner."

She leaned back against the pillows, relaxed.

He was not sure he wanted her quite that relaxed. He thought about running his thumb down the side of her instep that he already knew was so tender, but resisted.

"My house in Zurich is old. Just as our business, it's been in my family for generations. When my father died, neither of my sisters wanted it. Mia said it was haunted, and Emma was worried about her children destroying the antiques. I couldn't bring myself to move into the bedroom my mother and father had shared, so there I am, in my boyhood room.

"I'm planning a complete renovation, eventually, but I haven't gotten to it yet."

It occurred to him that the space called *home* was a low priority to him, linked in some way to the dangers he had revealed to Marlee last night.

The dangers of caring.

"Tell me about your family business," she invited.

Matteo found it so easy to talk to her.

"Family legend has it that it started hundreds of years ago on my mother's side, when my great-great-great-grandmother sold a handmade winter coat. And then another and another. Her name was Rosa, which coincidentally is also the name of Switzerland's highest peak.

"Over many generations, Monte Rosa Alpen Wear became a company that was known for extremely high-quality winter clothing, and a contract to supply an army with wool jackets moved it to the next level. And then it expanded into mountaineering and outdoor supplies and survival equipment.

"By the time my father took it over, the reputation of the company was cemented. But after the death of my mother, he took his hands off the reins. I think that though she stayed in the background, she was the detail person. Maybe even the driving force behind the company. Anyway, after her death, he wasn't watching the quality control. He wasn't interested in trends or how to stay current in an increasingly competitive market.

"My sisters and I watched helplessly as his indifference nearly drove the family business into the ground. Our four-hundred-year-old reputation was badly tarnished. We were getting reviews and complaints, and many of them said we were overpriced, old-fashioned, and skating on our name.

"I took marketing in university—that's where I met Mike. And by the time I was done, I knew exactly what needed to happen with Monte Rosa. I wanted my sisters involved. It seemed to me it had always been a women-driven company, even when men took the credit. So my sister Emma applied her brilliant design ideas to bring the clothing lines into this century, and Mia took over the quality control for the mountaineering and survival equipment lines. We dropped the *Wear* from the name and surged forward."

Matteo was aware he did not usually talk this much. It was very comfortable to talk to her. That was what he had wanted, wasn't it? Her comfort? But now it felt as if maybe it was too comfortable. The spell he'd tried to weave around her had spun back and caught him.

Because the next words out of his mouth shocked Matteo.

"I sometimes wonder, though I've never admitted it, if saving the family business made me feel as if I could save all that we were before my mother died."

"And did it?" Marlee asked softly.

"Not really," he admitted. "My father died before we began to enjoy the enormous success we have today."

He felt suddenly wildly uncomfortable with his confidences. He renewed his interest in the job at hand.

Matteo dabbed at Marlee's toenail. He frowned. It didn't really look like a flower. He tried to repair it. The brush slipped and a blob of white nail polish nearly obliterated her whole toe. He jumped up, relieved to be away from the intensity, and went in search of something to clean it off.

"I should have thought of this in advance," he muttered, feeling more composed when he came back. He wiped the botched nail polish.

"Toilet paper?" she said, the outlaw dancing in her eyes, and yet there was something right beneath that, too. Compassion. Concern. "I thought this was a classy joint."

He was grateful that she understood his need to move past what he had just said, to keep it light.

The nail polish was a perfect distraction. It had dried ever so slightly and his clumsy attempt to wipe it had left a cloudy smear on her toenail.

"So classy they hid the damned tissue. The nail polish brush is too big. I need something smaller. Aha!"

This was what got him through everything: razor focus, an ability to prioritize. And keep things—especially untidy things like feelings—in compartments.

He went into the suite and came back with a pen. He dipped the tip in the polish. And carefully put a single drop on her toe. Still a blob!

He scowled, wiped it off, dabbed again.

"Quit laughing," he told her sternly, "it makes your toe shake."

"I can't help it. I feel like Cleopatra."

Again, he felt grateful to her for moving on, for keeping it light between them, and shifting the topic away from his confession.

"And to think yesterday you were just an outlaw," Matteo said, in the same vein as her.

"I know. Quite a promotion in one day. Not only am I Cleopatra, but I have a slave."

"Ah," he said. "My queen, your wish is my command."

For a moment, she was very silent. He glanced up at her. His mouth went dry.

"I wish," she said softly, "that you could find what you're looking for."

He stared at her.

"I wish you could have your sense of family back. And safety."

He felt as if what he was looking for—the thing he had been searching for without knowing that he searched—was in her eyes, like a promise.

He looked away from her. He concentrated on the job in front of him. His hand didn't feel steady.

"There," he said, putting her foot away from him, and with it, hopefully, the sense of weakness and wanting that seemed to be enveloping him.

She pulled up her knees and inspected his work. Her suppressed mirth gave way. She gave a shout of laughter.

"I don't get what's so funny," he said gravely.

"It doesn't look like a flower. It looks like an octopus."

He retrieved her toe and studied it. "You might have something there, Queen Cleo. Call Fiona. Change the theme."

"Egyptian?" she suggested.

"Or Down by the Sea."

"Which theme will Henri fit into better?"

"Oh, Henri! Have you told her yet, about Henri?"

"Not yet. The time hasn't seemed right. She's a nervous wreck."

After all the hoops Fiona was making her

jump through, Marlee was still able to think what Fiona was going through?

He was not at all sure he had ever met anyone this big-hearted before.

It was a warning. She was too soft. Too tender.

A person like Marlee would be so easily hurt.

And yet, the impulse to kiss her foot was so great that he sprang to his feet.

"Well," he said, "our work here is done."

Her eyes went very wide.

He felt the sudden breeze on his bare skin.

He looked down, already knowing what he would see. The towel must have caught on the edge of the basket chair. It lay in a white puddle at his feet.

Matteo looked at Marlee, expecting to see her laughing now that the tables were turned and the embarrassing wardrobe malfunction moment was his.

But she was not laughing.

Matteo turned and dove in the pool.

CHAPTER THIRTEEN

MARLEE WATCHED THE faint splash as Matteo dove cleanly into the water and disappeared under its tranquil blue surface. She was unabashedly appreciative of him. He was quite gorgeous with no clothes on. He would make the perfect male specimen to carve in marble.

She found herself continually shocked by the surprises life held after she'd made that decision to be bold, and by the fact a different side of herself was being revealed.

For instance, if she was still the woman she had been when she arrived at Coconut Cay, she would get up now, go inside the villa and give Matteo an opportunity to exit the water and retrieve his towel and his dignity.

Instead, she got up and wandered to the water's edge. She stuck her toe in, just as he resurfaced, treading water. He shook droplets of water from his hair, scowling at her.

"Don't get your feet wet," he ordered her.

"I can if I want."

"You'll spoil the nail polish."

She smiled at him. "As if that's our biggest problem," she said sweetly.

His scowl deepened. "If you could just put my towel where I can reach it and turn your back for a moment, I'd be most grateful."

She leaned over and picked up his towel. She made a grave show of contemplating it thoughtfully. Then she tossed it behind her, well out of his reach.

"Hey! That isn't funny!"

"It is," she said. "Barely."

"Marlee, be reasonable."

"You thought it was hilarious when it happened to me."

"I didn't really."

"Where is all your European sophistication now?" she asked him. Slowly, deliberately, she moved her hand to the top button of her shirt. She flicked it open.

His eyes went wide.

She flicked open the next one.

He licked his lips. "Marlee, just pass me the towel. Before we—you—do something you regret."

"What would I regret?" she egged him on softly.

"Wrecking the nail polish!" he said, and she heard something desperate in his tone.

"It didn't look like a flower, anyway."

"If you'll just be reasonable, I'll try again. I'm sure I can master a flower—"

"I'm all done being reasonable," she interrupted him.

"No, you're not," he insisted.

She laughed. She was not sure she had ever felt her full feminine power quite so delightfully as when she slowly removed her top and let it slide from her hand to the pool deck.

Ever so slowly, she trailed her hand down over her belly to the button on her shorts. She undid them and stepped out of them.

If she expected sanity to hit her as the sultry tropical air caressed her skin, she was completely wrong.

She didn't feel shy at all. The woman who had run from the ocean trying to hide herself was gone forever. Wallflowers who inspired pity were banished from within herself!

Matteo had done this to her.

He was doing it to her now. The look in his eyes—desperation, hunger, appreciation—emboldened her. She was not who she had been before.

"What are you doing?" he croaked.

"I'm going skinny-dipping."

"No, you're not!"

"But you're doing it."

"By accident!"

"I bet it feels wonderful."

"It doesn't."

"The water right up against your skin, no barriers. I'm curious."

"You've experienced that every single time you've taken a bath."

"I don't think it's the same."

"It is."

She smiled at him, then she reached behind her own back and flicked open the clasp on her bra. It fell away. Nothing awkward about it at all. She stretched up and enjoyed the sensation of sun on her naked skin.

Matteo groaned, an almost animal sound of suffering.

"Imagine that," she said. "I'm twenty-six years old, and I've never felt the sun on my breasts before. I could get used to it, I think."

"Marlee," he said hoarsely, "you are killing me."

She smiled more deeply at him. "But what a way to go, right?"

She stepped out of her panties and then jumped off the edge of the deck way out into the pool. She felt the water close over her head.

For a split second, she enjoyed the sensation of warm water, silky, against her naked skin. It was just as she had hoped. Utterly freeing. Unbelievably sensual.

But then her feet did not find the bottom of the pool. She had not thought she was going in the deep end. A little too late, she remembered she was not a very good swimmer.

Marlee realized, panic beginning, that she was in way over her head, in every possible way.

Her feet finally found the bottom of the pool. She hated opening her eyes underwater, but she did.

It seemed as if the light was a long way away. She pushed against the floor of the pool and rocketed to the surface. She drew in a single, strangled breath, and managed one distressed yelp. She flapped her arms frantically and struck out for the safety of the side.

But gravity was winning. Panic made her limbs heavy.

And then safety found her.

If it could be called that.

Matteo's arms closed around her, and she twined her arms around his neck.

"Hang on," he said. "I've got you."

Had more beautiful words ever been spoken?

"Relax," he told her, his voice deep and calm and soothing in her ear. Effortlessly, he moved them to shallower water.

"You can stand now," he said.

But somehow, she could not let go. And somehow, they were not safe.

Probably the farthest thing from it.

She looked up into his face, so familiar to her already. And in some way that was beyond explanation, given the shortness of their acquaintance, beloved.

Maybe that was what happened when someone saved your life.

She traced the wet surface of his face with her fingertips, hungry to know his brow, his eyelids, the straight line of his nose, the cleft of his chin. He moved his head until his lips found her questing fingers.

One by one, as he tasted them, she gloried in the larger sensation of their bodies touching, wet skin slippery as silk connecting them both.

His hand moved to the back of her head, and he drew her face to his. His mouth found her mouth.

There was no tentativeness in either of them. No hesitation.

This kiss had none of the innocence of the kiss she had bestowed on him yesterday after their adventure.

Though it was everything that kiss had hinted it could be. There was savagery and sweetness combined as Marlee was engulfed by sensation.

Every cell in her awakened to Matteo's quest, Matteo's call. Every part of her, from the tips of her toes to the tips of her hair, tingled and sparked. It was as if her desire had been a dying ember at her core and was now flickering to life, after a breath of air had found it.

The breath intensified. A breeze. And the ember of desire within Marlee flared, glowing red hot. Just when it seemed it could not become any more intense, as if the heat could consume her, Matteo dropped his head to her breast.

That fire within took hold, roared to life.

It felt as if the water should boil around them.

He lifted her easily and carried her from the water. The sensation in the pit of her stomach was deeply primal, as if she was the woman a warrior had come home to. He kicked open the door of the villa with his foot and took her through to the coolness to the master suite, his easy strength stealing her breath.

He laid her on the center of the bed, and she felt herself sinking into the deep comfort of its snowy whiteness.

Matteo stood above her, looking down. He waited, his eyes drinking her in, for a signal from her. She noticed everything: the water droplets on his lashes, the plump line of his bottom lip, the broadness of his shoulders, the deepness of his chest, his ribs marching down his sides to the narrowness of his waist.

The woman she used to be—yesterday, though

it felt as if it was a hundred years ago—put up a faint fight.

Think, the old Marlee implored her.

About what? the new Marlee asked.

Consequences. Tomorrow.

But none of that mattered. There was no tomorrow, and the consequence of not following her heart seemed as if it would be the worst one of all.

A form of death.

The kind of nonlife—dull as a rump-sprung recliner in front of a TV—that she had accepted for far too long.

She opened her arms to him.

And everything within Marlee sang.

Live.

And so she lived.

Matteo was an exquisite lover. He wanted her pleasure. He teased. He tantalized. He found each of her ticklish secrets—particularly that delicate instep—and tormented her with them.

And he coaxed her to open a thus unexplored side of herself. She experimented. She indulged. She risked.

Much later, they lay in a tangle of sheets and the glow of utter fulfillment, splashes of sunshine striping them in light filtered green from the thick foliage outside his window.

Then they showered together, learning the

textures and secrets of each other's bodies all over again. He shampooed her hair, something in the tenderness of his touch exquisitely possessive.

You belong to me.

And then they dried each other off, kisses following the path of the towel.

And then reality knocked.

Literally.

Someone was hammering on the villa door.

They both froze, silent.

"Hey, Matt," Mike called through the closed door. "What's up? You coming golfing?"

Marlee stifled a giggle. Matteo put a hand on her arm. As if that was necessary. She was hardly going to go throw open the door!

Mike knocked again, and then they heard other male voices join his, jovial. And then they moved on, their voices drifting away.

"Go golfing," Marlee told him, casually, as if it didn't matter to her one little bit. As if she was suave and sophisticated and did things like this all the time.

Not once in a lifetime.

But she was holding her breath and Matteo was not the least fooled.

"You think I would go golfing after that?" He laughed, and his laughter filled her to the brim.

"Come on," he said, "Let's get dressed. I am

not wasting one minute that I could spend with you. What do you want to do?"

She started breathing again.

Be with you. That was it. All of it.

"What I don't want to do," she said carefully, "is risk running into Fiona." She shuddered inwardly at the thought of the grilling that could ensue if the bride saw them together.

"Or Mike," he agreed.

What had happened between them felt raw and real and as if a neon sign was blinking above them announcing their newfound intimacy: *lovers.*

Marlee could not bear the thought of sideways looks, smiles, conjecture, interrogation. For a while longer, she wanted this just to belong to her and Matteo. She wasn't ready to share it with their circle of friends.

Especially her friends.

Who saw her as prim and controlled, always the stable one, always the responsible one. They would be utterly shocked to see her now.

How would she and Matteo get through the rehearsal dinner?

But that was tonight and that seemed a long way away. Only this moment seemed to exist, glittering, sparkling, infused with their newfound awareness of each other.

So much so that it was hard to keep their

hands off each other as they made their way to the resort gate, both of them stealing furtive looks about, not ready just yet to have their togetherness spotted. Confronted. *Challenged.*

Outside the gates of the resort, Marlee heaved a huge sigh of relief.

She felt gloriously free. The street—vegetable stands and trinket booths and chickens and cars and children in school uniforms—shone with a spectacular light.

And then she saw the donkey cart, parked at the curb, waiting sleepily for passengers. It felt as if even the universe was on their side, providing a perfect getaway plan for them, two outlaws of love on the run.

CHAPTER FOURTEEN

"Look," Marlee said to Matteo, taking his arm and tugging him toward the ancient and colorful cart, "It's Mackay with Henri and Calamity."

"It's obviously Mackay, but how do you know which donkeys those are? He could have a whole herd of donkeys, for all you know."

"Are you skeptical of my ass expertise?" Marlee asked. She let her hand graze ever so lightly—possessively—over the back of Matteo's shorts.

She relished the unexpected direction of her life: she was teasing her lover on the colorful main street of an exotic island.

"I consider myself something of an expert now, on ass…ets. Having been exposed, so to speak." She leveled him a look and wagged her eyebrows at him.

He rewarded her with his laughter, that rich deep sound that she could live the rest of her life trying to coax from him. Even more precious was the slight blush.

"Right, Mackay? Henri and Calamity?"

"That's right." Mackay tipped his hat to them

as if he had been waiting for them to appear. His glance went between them and he grinned, as if he *knew*—probably from Matteo's blush—that the romance he had predicted for *maybe after lunch* yesterday had unfolded.

To Marlee, his knowing look confirmed the wisdom of them leaving the resort.

"I knew it was Henri immediately because of his cute ears," Marlee told Matteo. "Calamity is sporting a pink feather headdress to let the world know she's a girl."

She went and bestowed each of the donkeys a kiss on their furry, soft noses.

"Miss Marlee. Mr. Matteo. Where can Mackay take you?"

"Where to?" Matteo asked her.

"Anywhere. No plan is a good plan."

Matteo snapped his fingers and turned to Mackay. "We need somebody who can do a pedicure."

"Really?" Marlee said, wiggling her toes and gazing at them. "I kind of like the octopus. It's growing on me."

"It's not faring well after the pool. And the other activities."

It was her turn to blush. And then he was laughing again and her laugher joined his.

"I'm not willing to spoil a perfect day by risk-ing the wrath of Fiona," Matteo decided. "I've already missed the scheduled golf event, so let's make sure we pass pedicure inspection."

Marlee felt a little disappointed. She had hoped for something a bit more romantic.

But then he leaned close to her and said in her ear, "I'm going to watch very closely so I get it just right next time."

Next time.

"I think you got it just right last time," she said huskily.

"I'm talking about the pedicure," he said.

"Oh, *that.*"

And there it was between them: that sizzling connection.

"You know someone, Mackay?" Matteo asked. "Who can paint Marlee's toenails?"

"Yes, yes, my cousin." He regarded them sagely for a moment. "There are all kinds of hunger."

Evidence they were practically telegraphing what had just happened between them.

"But perhaps some food first?"

"Absolutely," Matteo said.

And so they found themselves at the kind of place Marlee would *never* have gone to. It was an off-the-beaten-track establishment that tourists did not find. It was part roadside stand and part house. A picnic area, packed with locals, had been cordoned off on the street and cars steered cheerfully around it. As soon as they sat down, three men appeared on a makeshift stage.

The joyous shouts and sounds of calypso filled the air as Marlee and Matteo fed each other spicy local food off their fingertips.

"I think this may be the most delicious food I've ever eaten," Marlee said with a satisfied sigh when the plates in front of them were empty.

"Or your senses might be heightened," Matteo said in her ear.

Might be?

She hadn't had a single thing to drink beyond water and yet she felt intoxicated. Marlee could feel all of life tingling against her skin. As if she was breathing in the colors and sounds of Coconut Cay until they were part of her.

Her eyes fell on him.

Matteo.

Part of her.

And no matter what happened next, part of her forever.

Not that she was going to spoil one second of this by asking herself what could possibly happen next.

But what happened next was astonishing.

Mackay bowed before her. "Would you dance with me, Miss Marlee?"

She cast a look over his shoulder. A space had

been cleared and people were up on the make-shift dance floor.

The music had become even more lively. People clapped and sang along. A spontaneous party had erupted.

"I don't—"

She was about to say she didn't dance. And she particularly didn't dance like *that*.

But that was the old Marlee. The wallflower. The object of people's pity.

The new Marlee was open to all the invitations life threw at her. After just a moment's hesitation, she kicked off her sandals, took Mackay's extended hand and allowed him to lead her out onto the now quite crowded dance area.

The lyrics of the song were unabashedly sexual.

I want you,
I want you moving against me,
I want your heart to beat against mine,
I want you, I want you, I want you.
I want to intertwine.

Marlee stood frozen to the spot. She looked at the people around her. So free. So uninhibited. Celebrating the sensual part of themselves and life.

She closed her eyes. She felt the primal beat of the music stir within her.

She lifted her hands over her head and swayed. Almost of their own accord, her hips did a slow circle. The music caught her and carried her.

Marlee was aware that she felt more fully a woman than she had ever felt in her life. She danced in recognition of her softness. She danced in celebration of her curves. She danced in honor of her rightful place in the cycle of life.

She realized she might be dancing *with* Mackay, but she was dancing *for* Matteo.

Matteo watched Marlee dancing.

She delighted him. From teasing him about asses, to kissing donkeys, to this.

Something in her had been unleashed since they had made love, and all of it was extraordinarily beautiful to watch.

But now, as she danced, he could see the changes in her were remarkable. This was not the same woman who had stood outside in that fluffy dress defiantly contemplating smoking a cigar, as if by doing that she could erase what she so obviously was.

A little shy.

A little uptight.

And yet, even then, he had known something lurked beneath the surface.

And Marlee had unveiled that something for him in the last few hours. She was on fire with life.

It didn't feel as if she was becoming some-one else. Not at all. It felt as if she was peeling away layers of reserve, and underneath, with a light that outshone the sun, was the real Marlee.

Everyone seemed to see it. It was as if all the other dancers were orbiting around her brilliant light.

These, he decided, had been the best hours of his entire life.

As he watched her dance, Matteo became aware that something had stolen up on him and come to reside right in the region of his heart.

It had been so long.

Could it possibly be?

Yes.

Happiness.

In its purest and simplest form.

Not the flush of success, not the satisfaction of filling hours with production, not the rush of saving his family business. It was something more intrinsic than that.

The song stopped, and Matteo got to his feet. He was not a dancer. Had two left feet. And yet the dance was within him, calling him, insist-ing that, like Marlee, he acknowledge the ancient rhythms of life and his part in those rhythms.

And nothing could have stopped him from sharing his just-discovered happiness with Mar-lee, who was, after all, the source of it all.

Marlee and Matteo danced. They became part of a joyous conga line that stopped traffic and snaked in and out of local yards and stores. They participated in a spirited game of limbo, which, as it turned out, Marlee had a real gift for.

Matteo, not so much.

Finally, they had to acknowledge the time. With Marlee clutching her limbo trophy—a carved coconut—they waved goodbye to all their newfound friends and boarded the donkey cart. Mackay serenaded them as he drove.

Leaning against each other and hands intertwined, they enjoyed the clip-clop of the donkeys' hooves and Mackay's song. He brought them eventually to a tiny salon on a narrow back street, where children were playing with a ball and sticks.

The children stopped and thronged Mackay. Finally managing to put them aside, Mackay took Marlee and Matteo into the shop and introduced them to his cousin, Margaret. Marlee showed her the picture of the painted toenails on her phone, and Margaret indicated it would not be a problem to achieve that result.

"I'll watch." Matteo swept his hand toward Marlee's feet. "I made that mess. Next time I can do better."

Next time.

Tomorrow was the wedding.

And on Sunday they would all begin to go their separate ways. He had an important meeting in Zurich on Monday.

Marlee was watching him, and he could see it in her eyes, too. The questions about next time.

How could there not be a next time?

Margaret was frowning at Marlee's feet. She guided her to a row of rather elaborate-looking chairs, sat her down and slipped her sandals off. She shook her head at Matteo's handiwork and moved Marlee's feet into what seemed to be an ancient, but spotlessly clean, basin. She turned a switch and the basin bubbled to life.

"Oh, it's lovely," Marlee said, leaning back in the chair, relaxing.

"I told you feet soaking was a necessary step," Matteo reminded Marlee.

"Customers only," Margaret said sternly, pointing to a sign. The look on her face clearly said she didn't intend to make an exception.

Instead of leaving, he went and took the spa seat beside Marlee. He kicked off his shoes.

"Okay," he said. "I'll be a customer, too, then."

Margaret, obviously calculating the extra fee, looked quite pleased with this development. She turned on the basin at the foot of his chair and he lowered his feet in. Marlee was right. It was lovely.

Matteo looked around. The shop was very

clean, but everything, including Margaret's dress, was faded and worn, and the basin his feet were soaking in was making a whining noise.

What he saw was how poor Margaret was. But it was evident in the set of her chin and shoulders and in the meticulous tidiness of the shop that she was extremely proud.

"I'd like the donkey done, too. Not the girl one."

Margaret's mouth fell open.

So did Marlee's.

"He's to be in the wedding photos," Matteo explained. "It's important we all look our best."

Marlee's mouth closed and she regarded him thoughtfully. It was apparent she could see right through him. To be honest, Matteo wasn't sure that if having someone read you so accurately was a good thing or a bad thing.

Still, Marlee was smiling at him with a look that could make him want to get up in the morning and decide, every single day, how to be a better man.

Her hand came across the space between the two chairs and closed over his. When had life ever felt so right?

Margaret considered him for a moment, trying to decide if he was a crazy tourist pulling her leg.

"Dead serious," he told her, squeezing Marlee's hand. She squeezed back, a secret language between them.

"Expensive," Margaret warned him.

He nodded, and she went to a drawer and began pulling jars and jars of gold nail polish. At the door she shouted at the children, handed over the polish and pointed to the donkey.

"Don't forget the flowers," he called to her. Soon the sound of children laughing drifted in and filled the space of the tiny shop.

"I love that sound," Marlee said, settling back in her chair, a smile tickling the delicious curve of her lips. "It's better than music."

Matteo considered that. Marlee didn't just love that sound. She loved children. It felt like a warning trying to pierce the bubble of happiness around him. What was he doing, exactly?

CHAPTER FIFTEEN

THE QUESTION BUZZED around Matteo—what was he doing, exactly?—like a bothersome fly intent on ruining a perfect picnic.

"So," he said, carefully, "are you planning on having children someday?"

"Oh, yes," Marlee said. "I've even recently picked names."

Something like panic reared up in him. He'd thought—well, he wasn't sure what he'd thought—but certainly not about naming children!

And then she hooted at the look he could not keep from crossing his face.

"Henri and Calamity," she told him mirthfully.

She was letting him know that it was okay to keep it light. That it was okay not to think about the future.

But was it?

"Do you like it?" she asked. "Calamity for a little girl?"

"That's a terrible name for a child," he told her sternly, and yet it felt as if he could see a little

girl—all curls and mischief and green eyes—
who could live up to that name.

A shy assistant appeared and began working
alongside Margaret, and it was easy to follow
Marlee's lead, to dismiss pressing questions, to
just be here enjoying the sensations and the nov-
elty of it all.

It was easy to press Mute on the warning bells
that wanted to spoil everything.

Matteo and Marlee's feet were removed from
the basins and carefully dried. Matteo then
watched in fascinated horror as the two women
plugged in apparatuses that looked for all the
world like miniature circular saws with cement-
cutting blades in them.

"What are those?" he asked in an undertone
to Marlee.

"I'm not expert on pedicures but I think it's
some kind of defoliating device."

"If they pull down welding helmets, we'll
run," he said.

"I think we're at step two," Marlee decided.
"Remember from last night? Get rid of dead
skin."

"Last night you thought it was gross," he reminded her.

"These are professionals," she told him.

"Those look suspiciously like grinders," he said.

"Grinders?" Marlee asked.

"You know. They can grind paint off buildings with them. Destroy concrete. Cut nails in two, that kind of thing."

"Cut toenails in two?"

"Nail nails!"

"Don't worry," Marlee said, "they are not going to grind off your feet."

He wasn't so sure about that. The grinding apparatuses were coaxed to life. He discovered Marlee wasn't the only one with a ticklish instep.

"She's having her wicked way with my foot!" he said to Marlee.

"Is that trepidation I detect in your oh-so-fearless self?" Marlee teased him.

It felt wonderful to be teased by her, to leave the warning bells on silent, to enjoy her hand finding his and tightening on it.

"Be brave," she told him.

And somehow it didn't feel as if her instruction had anything to do with what was happening to his feet.

At all.

Marlee knew the exact moment she recognized the true danger of her fling with Matteo.

And it wasn't when she swam in the ocean with him, or rode behind him on a scooter, or let him paint her toenails. It wasn't when she'd decided to skinny-dip with him. Or when they had made wild, impetuous love together.

All that had deepened the attraction.

Inflamed her infatuation.

But when Matteo asked Margaret to paint the donkey's feet, too, the quiver that had been within her grew to a tremor that felt dangerous, like the pre-earthquake kind.

Because she knew exactly what he was doing.

It was more than apparent to her he was finding a way to be generous that still allowed Margaret her dignity.

Looking at him after he requested a pedicure for Henri, Marlee felt as if she could see him all the way to his soul.

And what she saw was innate kindness.

Decency.

A lovely kind of honor.

But then, because she could see those things, she saw the moment it turned on her.

So, are you planning on having children someday?

As if he could clearly see, despite everything she had become in the last few hours and days, that under all that boldness lurked a traditional girl with traditional dreams of family and forever.

Trapping dreams, if the expression on his face when she said she had already named the children, was any indication.

For once in her life, Marlee didn't want to think about the future. Or forever. She didn't want to complicate things with imagining repercussions or making moral judgments about right or wrong.

She didn't want her world to be predictable or rule-bound.

She just wanted to immerse herself in the delightful surprises that were being handed to her, moment after moment.

She would deal with the fallout, the inevitable devastation of the earthquake, later.

And who said there had to be fallout? Couldn't she just have a lovely fling like all the rest of the world was doing?

Of course she could.

An hour later, they were laughing together as they walked gingerly out to the donkey cart. They had been provided with cheap flip-flops and the toe separators were still in.

She had a perfect white flower on the fourth toenail of each foot.

He had opted for an octopus.

To the delight of the waiting children, they made a huge fuss over Henri's beautifully painted hooves.

And then, aware they had not left themselves

enough time, they urged Mackay to make haste back to the resort.

It was a wild ride as the donkeys clattered through the narrow streets, bouncing Marlee and Matteo into each other and making them hang on for dear life.

At the resort they quickly went their separate ways to get ready for the rehearsal. Thankfully, it wasn't a dress rehearsal!

The yellow sundress had been picked up off her floor, sent to the cleaners, and was now hanging, refreshed, off the shower bar in her bathroom.

Totally wrong, of course, for the rehearsal dinner. It drew too much attention. It was too loud. It was the bride's time to shine.

"That's tomorrow," Marlee told herself and slipped the dress over her head.

She arrived a few minutes late, breathless, and took her place beside Fiona, who threw her—and the dress—a faintly disapproving look.

In response she wagged her newly painted toes and actually earned a nod of approval.

"Love that color on you," Brenda said. It seemed perhaps a defiant reaction to Fiona's look. "You should wear bright colors more often."

"The length is very daring," Kathy chimed in. "I love it! You carry it perfectly. You look hot!"

And she obviously did not mean the melting-from-the-heat kind of hot.

The approval of her friends was really confirmation that Arthur had been right. Somewhere along the way she had become too muted, too comfortable and dull in the way she approached the ultra-predictable life that had made her feel safe, yes, but had also shut down parts of her.

She felt the moment of Matteo's arrival, the air shifting as he joined the wedding party on the beach. She looked everywhere but at him.

How could she look at him without their intimacy being obvious to every single person there?

Especially with the new dress, people might start arriving at conclusions!

Even knowing that, she could not stop herself. She slid a look at him.

He had put on shoes. He was dressed in a light pair of slacks and a shirt so hastily buttoned he had missed the top one.

Her eyes fastened on the part of his chest that she could see.

She remembered her hands on his naked flesh. He glanced at her. Some white-hot memory darkened the turquoise of his eyes to navy blue. They both looked away at exactly the same moment.

The rehearsal was a tense nightmare of trying not to look at him.

Trying not to touch him!

Thankfully, in the wedding party, he was coupled with Kathy, not her. They endlessly practiced gliding down the aisle, to Fiona's instructions.

"Kathy, just a little slower."

"Brenda, hold the flowers up a bit higher."

"Marlee, a little less swish."

Swish. She had become a hot girl in a yellow sundress who swished. She shot Matteo a look.

He was looking deliberately off into the distance. His lips were twitching.

"I think we should practice how we're lining up for the register signing one more time and we'll have it perfect," Fiona decided.

"Forget perfect," Mike said. "I'm famished. Let's eat!"

"But we need to talk about photos. That will happen in between the ceremony and the dinner."

Photos.

Marlee suddenly realized she had not broken it to Fiona yet about a donkey instead of a horse.

"I'm trying to decide if I'll wreck the dress or not. It's a hard decision. Such a nice dress to jump in the ocean with!"

"Decide over dinner," Mike said firmly. "Or

maybe don't even decide. You could just be spontaneous."

It felt as if he was speaking to Marlee about the donkey decision, not to Fiona about the photo decisions.

The very idea of being spontaneous seemed to appall Fiona.

No matter what happened next, Marlee thought, she would always be grateful for this: that Matteo had broken her away from her own rigid need for control.

And then, to Fiona's horror, the whole wedding party mutinied and stampeded toward the dinner that had been set up for them at the wedding venue, a private grotto just off the area marked for the beach ceremony.

It was stunningly beautiful, with a waterfall at one end, the deep greens of thick foliage forming walls of privacy around it. Cables of outdoor lights hung above tables already set up for tomorrow.

As waiters brought out dinner, other staff came and lit tiki torches that illuminated the dining area as well as the dance floor and bar.

Again, they rehearsed. The order of the toasts. The timing. Who would stand where, who would say what, what would make the best photos?

Matteo, appearing neither bored nor as if he

had other plans, rose from the table when Fiona finally stopped to catch a breath.

"It's been a long day," he said casually. "And I seem to have jet lag. In the interest of being nice and fresh for the wedding tomorrow, I'm going to head off."

After a suitable amount of time had passed, Marlee also got up.

"I seem to have a tiny headache." This was a bald-faced lie, but not being the woman she had been when she'd arrived at Coconut Cay, Marlee didn't feel even a little bit guilty. "I think, also in the interest of being at my best tomorrow, I'll turn in."

"But we haven't rehearsed cutting the cake yet. Or the first dances."

Once, Marlee would have sat back down.

But not now.

"You can fill me in tomorrow," Marlee said.

Once, Fiona would have argued with her. But now she scanned her face, and must have seen something different there, too.

On the other hand, maybe she thought all the wedding planning was making Marlee sad about her own missed day. Did Mike nudge Fiona?

"All right. But you have to be at my suite really early. There's so much to do."

"I promise I will be." There was so much to do. She had a dress that needed complete altering! But first things first. Marlee set off to find Matteo. His place? Hers? Their beach?

Before she could decide, a hand shot out of the darkened shrubbery and pulled her in. Her surprised cry was silenced by a very familiar hand.

"I thought you'd never leave," he whispered in her ear.

And then he kissed her. Thoroughly. Until she wondered if you could die from kisses. Or, more accurately, from wanting what the kisses promised.

Hand in hand, breathless with anticipation, neither of them acknowledging the end was near, they went to his villa.

And they didn't walk.

They ran.

CHAPTER SIXTEEN

MARLEE WOKE UP in a nest of sparkling white sheets, to the sounds of birds. They were loud as they celebrated the first rays of light that heralded the coming of the new day.

She was beside Matteo, sleeping on her side, one knee up, her hand splayed possessively across his beautiful chest.

It was the wedding day.

And she didn't feel sad at all. There was no longing for her own canceled day. In fact, it seemed like a perfect day to celebrate the glories of love.

She was aware she should feel exhausted. They had barely slept. They had so much to say to each other. It felt as if they needed to squeeze it all into one more day.

He had told her about his carefree days as a young boy, exploring the Alps with his father.

She had told him about her large, traditional family.

And then about Arthur, and the fact that her longing for the traditions of her family was so strong that she might have read qualities into his character that he didn't have, and accepted things in the relationship she should have never accepted.

She had told Matteo about practically being dumped at the altar.

Not as if she was telling him of a terrible tragedy, but as if it was a wonderful story about how something that seemed bad could turn into something good.

"My niece Amey likes gaming," Matteo had said to her. "She told me that in a game as soon as you hit trouble, or more bad guys, you know you're going the right way."

As she looked at his sleeping face now—so extraordinarily handsome, so beautifully familiar to her—Marlee had never been more certain that every single thing she had once judged as bad had just been a way of getting her life on the right path.

Still, as much as she would have liked to linger, taking in his face and the texture of his skin and the gorgeous male aroma of him, she had a great deal to do, and that was before factoring in Fiona's inevitable last-minute errands.

She left Matteo quietly, so as to not wake him. Then, bathed in the first pink stains of dawn, she made her way across the resort to her own cabana.

The morning seemed to shimmer with the same brilliant light that was shining within her.

She took the bridesmaid's dress down from where it was still hanging in the bathroom. She laid it out carefully. And then, using her handy sewing kit, she began to take the dress apart.

Finally done, she put on the dress.

Marlee looked at herself in the full-length mirror behind the bathroom door. She smiled.

Matteo's first waking thought was that Marlee wasn't there. He could feel her absence deeply, as if something essential was gone from his world.

He buried his nose in her pillow and let her fragrance fill him.

He thought of all the confidences they had exchanged last night. And the other things, too.

He was aware he could not wait to see her again, as if his life would not be complete until the moment he laid eyes on her.

As it turned out, that was at the wedding.

For the first time, as he gathered with Mike and the other members of the groom's party on the beach, he saw the payoff of all of Fiona's persnickety pursuit of perfection.

Because that was exactly what she had achieved. Perfection.

Framed by an arbor arch threaded through with gardenias was perfect white sand and an endless blue sea.

The guests were beginning to arrive and take their seats on the white chairs, a pink silk bow on the back of each.

Mike took his place under the arbor, and just as they had rehearsed—who would have ever thought Matteo would be grateful for that endless rehearsal, but he was—they lined up beside him.

For a panicked moment, Matteo thought he might have been so besotted with Marlee that he'd forgotten the ring. He felt in his pocket and drew in a deep breath. No, there it was.

The notes of a piano filled the air. It wasn't a recording. He noticed the real piano and he had to give kudos to Fiona. The music rising to join the lap of waves and the call of birds could not be more beautiful.

Kathy, the maid of honor, came through a break in the hedge and walked—glided—through the sand and up the aisle between the chairs. He recognized the color of that dress.

Behind her came Brenda, and again, the color triggered his memory of the first time he had seen Marlee.

And then—his mouth dropped, and he quickly slammed it shut—came Marlee.

She was wearing the same dress that he had first met her in. Except that it wasn't the same dress at all.

The neckline had been altered, and the sleeves removed. Every puff and every ruffle had been stripped from it.

It clung to her like mist, and Marlee carried herself like a queen. Matteo was not sure he had ever seen a dress that so perfectly revealed the beauty and the boldness of the person who was wearing it.

Her hair was piled up on top of her head, and her makeup showed off everything about her, the height of those cheekbones, the bow of her mouth, and especially the depth and mystery held in those green eyes.

He felt as if everything faded, except her.

But then the subdued gasp of the crowd made him draw his eyes away from her. Fiona had entered the pathway.

Her dress and veil were extraordinary, but it was the light in her face that kept everyone's gaze on her.

Matteo glanced at Mike.

And felt pure envy for the look on his best friend's face.

Matteo was shocked by what he felt next.

A kind of devastation. *This* was what Marlee deserved. A man prepared to commit to her.

A man ready to devote his life to making her dreams come true. A man who wanted a future that held only her.

Last night, lying in the circle of his arms, she had told him who she really was and what she really needed.

Instead, what had Matteo given Marlee?

An affair.

A surrender, not to all the things she deserved, all the things that she had revealed to him last night she longed for—like tradition and family— but to base impulses.

He knew now what he didn't know then. She'd been betrayed by love. And still, she had come to him with hope.

She had never said that. That she *hoped*.

But he knew her now, and he knew she hoped for all the things a woman like her would hope for: a fairy-tale ending. Something with the word *forever* in it.

What he had given her, he thought, shocked, was a place that did not honor her.

Or himself.

Look at how they had been the day they had first made love. Hiding from their friends, as if they had something to be ashamed of.

Marlee arrived at the arbor. She looked at him. A smile, with their every intimacy in it, was directed at him.

Apparently she was not going to hide any-more. The dress said that.

And neither was he.

It was never too late to be a better man, Mat-teo decided then and there. Or even the best man, just like he was at this wedding.

He could become worthy of all that they had shared.

He could become worthy of this remarkable woman who had trusted him—of all people—with her broken self.

Fiona arrived at the altar and handed off her bouquet. She and Mike joined hands and faced each other.

The ceremony went off as practiced. It was flawless and without a hitch. They kissed to thunderous approval from those gathered to wit-ness the miracle of love.

Her bouquet was handed back to her, and the bride and groom moved off to the side where a white cane desk had been set up on the beach. They signed the register, and then Fiona gath-ered her bouquet and stood to one side.

As the piano played on, each member of the wedding party took their turn signing the doc-uments.

But then, just as that was finishing, the air was split with an ear-piercing bray.

Down the same path that the bridal party had walked down, came Mackay leading Henri.

The donkey was obviously angry. He was kicking his nicely painted back hooves to the side, nearly hitting the chairs. The guests were diving out of their seats to get out of his way.

Matteo abandoned the wedding party and raced down the aisle to help Mackay. "What's wrong?"

"He's missing Calamity," Mackay told him tightly. "They've never been apart. I couldn't even load him in the trailer without her. Listen."

Matteo cocked his head.

He could hear a smashing sound from the resort parking lot, located right above this entrance to the beach.

"It's Calamity," Mackay said. "In the trailer. By herself. Love-stricken."

Matteo listened to one final smashing sound. And then, not even his strength and Mackay's combined could hold the love-maddened Henri, who broke free of them, turned and stampeded up the aisle, back the way he had come.

But now, Calamity burst in through the hedge.

The donkeys raced toward each other. They skidded to a halt. They rubbed noses. They kicked up their heels, turned and ran down the path through the arbor, which was not wide enough for both of them to be side by side. It toppled. The minister sprang out of the way. The wedding party scattered. Mike threw himself on top of Fiona to protect her from the rampaging donkeys.

CHAPTER SEVENTEEN

HENRI AND CALAMITY cavorted up and down the beach braying loudly and kicking up their heels.

And then, suddenly, they were done.

As if they had created no mischief at all, they clomped back to Mackay, and sending him looks that could be interpreted as faintly apologetic, began to feast on the bridesmaids' bouquets that had been abandoned on the cane registration table.

Mike helped Fiona up out of the sand.

The decision to wreck the dress seemed as if it might have been made for her. It was crushed and had sand ground into it.

It felt as if the whole world had gone still, every single person focused on her.

Matteo, like everyone else, held his breath.

Waiting.

For tears.

For a tantrum.

For the bride to express the inevitable frustration at the moment she had built to for so long being ruined.

Instead, as Fiona stared up at Mike, her expression softened with tenderness. She looked at her new husband with an expression of pure wonder on her face.

"You saved me," she said, brushing at his suit jacket. "You put my life ahead of your own."

"That might be overstating it a bit," Mike said. Matteo could see how his friend's pragmatic nature was the perfect foil for Fiona's more dramatic one.

"What on earth is going on here?" Mike asked, running a hand through his hair. "Donkeys? Seriously?"

They all watched as Henri and Calamity contentedly finished off the bridesmaids' bouquets, flower stems dripping from their mouths.

"Um," Marlee offered, "the one on the right is Henri. He's here for the photos."

"But he's not a horse," Fiona said, a frown creasing her brow. Matteo wondered if perhaps they were going to have their bride meltdown moment, after all.

"Don't tell him," Marlee suggested in a stage whisper, and then, as a distraction, "Look at his hooves!"

Fiona crept a little closer to the donkey and looked.

And then, the best thing of all happened.

She beamed. And then Fiona laughed. Henri

noticed her—or more accurately her bouquet—and shuffled over. She held it out to him.

Now the perfect gentleman, Henri bobbed his head and nibbled his acceptance of the bride's offering.

"Best wedding moment *ever*," one of the guests said.

And the beach reverberated with sounds of applause that rivaled the enthusiastic approbation that had been given to the first kiss.

One thing about getting disaster out of the way early, Marlee decided, was that everyone relaxed after that.

The worst had already happened.

Except it wasn't really the worst.

It was just one of those obstacles that showed you that you were probably on the right path.

Marlee thought if she lived to be a hundred she would never forget the look on Fiona's face when she had gazed at her groom after he had thrown his body over her to protect her from perceived harm.

The donkeys also broke the ice as the guests swarmed them, making a fuss and taking pictures. Laughter filled the gathering and everyone was engaged with each other.

Marlee had a feeling the wedding photos—both the spontaneous ones and the official ones—were going to be the best ever. Award-worthy, no doubt.

Or maybe it was just that her own feelings were painting everything around her in shades of joy.

Because something had shifted between her and Matteo, too. How they felt about each other didn't feel as if it should be kept a secret anymore.

It didn't feel as if it *could* be kept a secret anymore.

It was spilling out of them. In the way they looked at each other. In the way they found excuses to touch each other. In the way they laughed together.

By the time the meal was done and the toasts completed and the dancing began, it felt as if they had sent out announcement cards.

Lovers.

Marlee danced with him the way she had danced to the sounds of calypso at the street restaurant.

She came into herself.

He had eyes only for her. He acted as though he were enchanted.

And he was so darned sexy! She could not wait to claim him as her own again tonight. And then, they would talk about the future. What they would do after they left Coconut Cay. How they would work out the challenges and logistics of meeting.

He had a *jet*. That should make everything easier.

The laughter nearly bubbled out of her.

Marlee Copeland was in love with a man with a jet.

Love.

Despite the party going in full swing around her, everything in her went still. It was way too soon for that. Wasn't it? But she had never felt this way before.

Not ever.

Not even when she'd been planning on marrying another man.

Who had, she reminded herself, walked away from her. If she felt this way about Matteo after just a few days, how was it going to feel when he came to his senses? When the magic they had experienced here was but a distant memory?

This wasn't the real world.

Not one single thing they had experienced here had anything to do with their real lives. He was the man with the jet, the international business tycoon.

She was the unexciting librarian from Seattle.

The thoughts threatened to crush the joy that was bubbling in her.

You didn't go from Arthur Drabeck to Matteo Keller. In the real world a woman like her didn't have a hope with a guy like this. Who did she think she was?

Love? Matteo had never mentioned the word *love*. Why would he? She, hopelessly naive, had fallen for a man who was enjoying a tryst with a willing partner. He knew the rules. He moved in a superfast world that included a jet and topless beaches. A world that she probably couldn't even imagine.

It was she who was breaking the rules by falling for him. By wanting more than he had ever offered.

The devastating fact was, once they stepped out of this bubble, it was over.

But she was not going to be devastated. Not just yet. In the days and weeks ahead, there would be plenty of time for that.

But now, Marlee decided, *this* was her moment. It felt as much like it was her moment as it was Fiona's.

This was the pinnacle of her whole life.

Right now.

This time she would be the one to walk away, before reality set in and Matteo realized the humiliating truth. It had been a fairy tale few days. She had become something she wasn't really. It was inevitable that he would come to realize that.

How much better to leave it like this? On a high note? Everything about them shimmering and untarnished? His memory of her of someone far bolder and more exciting than she really was or could ever hope to be.

She allowed the music back into that moment of utter stillness. She danced, immersed in the intensity of the experience. She knew they were counting down to midnight.

And then, the princess he had made her became an ordinary woman again.

The coach became a pumpkin.

The frills would probably magically reappear on her dress!

But regardless, it would be over. She had to make certain of that. She had to leave with her dignity intact, not as a woman who had lost her heart.

She danced as she wanted Matteo to remember her. She was uninhibited, sexy, sure of herself.

She danced as a woman who was memorizing every single thing about him. The way his eyes held hers, the curve of his lips, the flop of his hair over his brow, the utter sexiness of the way he moved.

The feeling of bliss, with its counterpoint of loss, was exhilarating and excruciating at the same time.

Be brave, she ordered herself, when the sense of loss would try to overwhelm her. *Just for a little while longer.*

She intended to make the next moments the best of her life. Given what the last few days had held, she was aware that was quite the challenge she had set for herself.

As if the universe understood the momentous occasion of a goodbye, the music slowed and the love song that played was heartbreaking and romantic.

His arms closed around her. He pulled her against himself.

She felt the heat of his body and the beat of his heart. She felt his breath on her hair, and his hand on the small of her back.

She breathed in his scent, hoping to take it in deeply enough that it became part of her, so she could remember it forever.

The music ended.

She reached up and took his lips with her own.

She tasted him as deeply as one human being could taste another. She savored him. She memorized him. She drew his essence deep into herself, an ember to warm her on the cold days of winter ahead.

A chime rang.

Smiling—the tears would come later—she took a step back from him.

"It's midnight," she said. "And I'm Cinderella. The ball is over."

And then she turned. She forced herself not to run, but to walk away from him slowly, not looking back. Unlike the fairy tale, there was no glass slipper to leave as a clue for him to follow.

Because life was not, after all, anything like the fairy tales.

CHAPTER EIGHTEEN

STUNNED, MATTEO WATCHED as Marlee walked regally past the staff carrying in trays of food for the midnight snack. The darkness of the tropical night folded around her, and she was gone.

What the hell had just happened?

The taste of her was still on his lips, and it felt as if the imprint of her body was seared into his own.

He went to follow her, and then he stopped himself.

Obviously, she was being the sensible one. They needed a cooling-off period. *He* needed a cooling-off period.

Just hours ago, he'd been thinking he'd done it all wrong. That he had dishonored her. That he had needed to do things differently. That he *would* do things differently. What did he think he should do instead? Ask her to marry him?

Insanity.

She'd been right to walk away.

They'd known each other *days.*

But it really bothered him that while he had, apparently, completely lost his mind, she still had good sense about her.

So, no, he was not going to chase her.

Marlee was right. It had been a fairy tale, but she was wrong if she thought she was the one under the spell! This island, from the moment he had walked down that path and found her on it, had put him under an enchantment.

It felt urgent to get away from here, to be restored to the person he had been a few short days ago. Then, maybe he'd be able to do what he did best. What people counted on him to do. What he was famous for, really.

Make a rational decision.

Not be swept along by the powerful currents of attraction and emotion.

Mike appeared in front of him. The look on his face warned Matteo he was not the only one whose magical evening had just come crashing to an end.

"Fiona's just had devastating news," Mike said quietly. "Her mother's had a heart attack. It's serious. Our flight isn't scheduled until late tomorrow afternoon. Even with extenuating circumstances, I'm pretty sure there's only the one flight out every day."

Matteo gave one final look at where Marlee had disappeared, and he drew in a deep breath. There.

Who was he kidding?

He couldn't have resisted the temptation of going to her if she was only steps away from him.

He probably would have ended up *begging*.

The thought was repulsive to him. It was an *attraction*. He was not powerless over it. And he especially wouldn't be powerless over it if he put some distance—physical distance and lots of it—between them.

Selfishly, he realized Fiona and Mike's crisis had just become his perfect escape.

"I'll take you," Matteo said to Mike. "We can use the jet."

Mike tilted his head at him. "You know, I still think of you as my college roommate, that guy who could figure out how to suspend a car from the bottom of a bridge with a budget of zero. I totally forgot there was a jet."

This was what Matteo loved about being with old friends.

His college buddies, in particular, rarely saw the trappings he'd accumulated. Instead, they saw just him.

And oddly, even though she knew of the trappings, it felt as if Marlee had never seen them, either. Just him.

And yet there she was, walking away.

What did that say?

"Thank you," Mike said. "We can be ready right away. We'll just grab passports and essentials. I'll ask the other members of the wedding party to pack up the rest of our stuff and get it home."

As he and Mike gathered a nearly hysterical Fiona and shepherded her toward the plane, Matteo knew it was better this way. Marlee had referenced a fairy tale. They had been on their own cloud, out of touch with reality, for days. Time for the landing, painful as that promised to be.

For one of the world's most respected businessmen, he did not think he had made a rational decision almost since his arrival on this tiny cay.

Except maybe one. This one. To be of service to his friends in their time of need.

Was he being of service? Or was he escaping the enchantment that had held him captive?

In less than an hour, Matteo had tossed his few items into a bag, a flight plan had been filed and they were onboard. Fiona sat in a forward seat. Mike snapped the belt for her. She was still in her wedding gown, covered in a blanket, shivering despite the warmth still seeping through the open cabin door.

"Who doesn't invite their own mother to their wedding?" she whispered. "I was worried she'd wreck it. I deserve this."

Mike made a shushing sound like one might use to comfort a child. "It's lucky she wasn't here. A hotel isn't the best place to have a heart attack."

Fiona seemed to consider it, and it seemed to bring her comfort.

Mike put his arms around her and she sighed into his chest.

But her pain reminded Matteo of the loss of his own mother.

It reminded him, starkly, of the danger of loss always lurking in the corridors, waiting to strike at the most unexpected moments.

As Matteo looked out the window, the lights of Coconut Cay, the safest place on earth, winked off one by one, until the island was lost in a sea of darkness.

He was aware of the irony. It was not, for him, the safest place on earth. The most dangerous thing of all had happened to him here.

The protective layer he had built around his heart had fallen away.

And love had crept past those broken barriers.

Matteo contemplated that word.

Love.

He looked over at the sobbing Fiona and re-membered his father.

His father had been one man before the loss of his mother, and another after. His father had fallen on the sword that was hiding in love's cloak.

He couldn't possibly love Marlee, Matteo told himself sternly. They barely knew each other.

And yet that did not feel like the truth, at all.

Which made this quick exit a blessing in dis-guise. What would knowing her longer do to him?

And then his memory dredged up this: his family picnicking on a wildflower-strewn hillside in the Alps.

His mother was chasing his sisters through the meadow, and shrieks of laughter filled the air.

He and his father were on the picnic blanket, and his father's eyes followed his mother as if he was unable to look away.

People said we were foolish. We got married within weeks of meeting. But you just know.

You just know, Matteo thought, like a fatal flaw that ran through the family. And then he reached for his headphones. To shut out the sounds of Fiona weeping softly.

And the weeping of his own heart as it broke in two.

So, Marlee thought as she packed up Fiona's belongings, she'd been wrong.

Because she had thought the donkey debacle had meant that a wedding disaster had been gotten out of the way early.

Of course, that was based on a thoroughly naive assumption that life was fair.

The truth was that disaster was random. There was no catastrophe roster, where some benign being checked his list and said, *Oh, I see they've already had their run of bad luck. No more for them. Their quota is used up.*

Now Matteo was flying Fiona and Mike home. They were already gone. Marlee had heard the roar of the jet engine split the quiet of the night.

It meant there were no second chances. Maybe part of her had hoped he would follow her and return the symbolic slipper, after all.

But there were fairy tales, and then there was reality, and reality had returned with a vengeance.

Brenda came into the room. "I just heard from Fiona. Her mother survived the night. I guess it's still touch and go, though."

"I'm glad they got there in time."

"Thanks to your dreamboat."

Marlee shot her a look. Was there just the slightest sarcastic emphasis on *your*? Or were her insecurities making her read things that weren't meant?

And yet, just beneath those insecurities, was there a new strength, too?

Marlee might have been kidding herself about Matteo, but something felt real and true about the woman she had become.

She intended to find out what was true about herself, and those few days with Matteo were what had given her the courage to do that.

To be what she had never been before this time on Coconut Cay.

Brave.

And that was the one ingredient that she had come to know was absolutely required to live a life fully.

Seattle, in November, was probably the dreariest city in the world. Weather roiled up and off the Pacific. The rain fell in ice-cold sheets. Clouds, gray and ominous, shrouded the nearby mountains. After the warmth and colors of Coconut Cay, the November nastiness should have seemed even worse than it normally did.

But the strange thing for Marlee was that it did not seem nasty.

Seattle—maybe her whole life—felt as if she had sleep-walked through it, and now she was wide-awake.

She had expected she might return from her romantic rendezvous on Coconut Cay to find herself more reserved, more fade-into-the-background, more insecure, more rigid in the habits that made her feel safe and secure in the world.

Instead, she was seeing the whole world with different eyes.

Marlee was well aware that she could have felt broken.

But that she didn't.

Some might say she made a choice to be brave instead of broken, but she didn't feel she was making choices so much as acknowledging she was changed in some fundamental way that made her embrace *everything*.

She found herself chatting with neighbors she had ignored in the past. She walked in the rain with no umbrella, loving how it soaked her hair. She said yes to a kayak lesson at a local pool from an expert who had presented at the library.

Fiona's mom, Mary, was released from the hospital, and Marlee dropped by and enjoyed reminiscing with her about the old neighborhood.

Marlee deepened other friendships with women at work and in her book club. And Fiona's rocky relationship with her family—and her close call with her mother—made Marlee appreciate her own family more.

She spent time with her mom and dad, appreciative of the solidness of their relationship, even as she realized the safety of it no longer appealed to her.

She made a full stop at a colorful poster that appeared in the library foyer one morning. It was advertising dance classes, and Marlee pulled off one of the tabs with a phone number on it.

And then she actually called it!

And then she actually signed up for dance classes. And loved them!

She thought missing Matteo would go away. They had only known each other for a few days.

But it didn't. She ached for him: to share these stories with him, to make new stories with him at her side.

One day, she was straightening a closet when the suitcase she had taken to the wedding on Coconut Cay fell off the top rack. After she put it back, she noticed something on the floor.

She picked it up.

It was the cigar. She held it to her nose, then ever so tentatively touched it to her tongue. Had she hoped she would taste Matteo on it?

She did not. Only the sweet, smoky taste of the wine the cigar had been dipped in. She thought of the woman she had been that night, and it was almost like looking at a stranger, and a childlike one, at that.

Had she really believed that sipping rum and toying with a cigar could change everything about you? She tucked the cigar into her bedside table.

As the dreary days of November turned to December, she still wished, every single day, that he would get in touch.

And when he didn't, she celebrated what he had given her: a verve for life that was like nothing she had ever felt before.

Fiona called and asked her to attend her and Mike's Christmas party.

Marlee's heart nearly stopped.

Would Matteo be there?

Of course he wouldn't! Not even international jet-setters flew to another country just for a Christmas party, did they?

"I know why you're hesitating," Fiona said.

"You do?" Marlee thought of how she had kissed Matteo at midnight and felt her cheeks burn.

But she wasn't sure it was with embarrassment. Maybe passion.

"I was awful," Fiona said. "A horrible person. Mike says he's surprised I have any friends left, and I'm darned lucky he married me. But he's forgiven me, because I have the best excuse ever. Can you guess?"

"Oh! Are you—"

"Yes! Pregnant. A complete surprise! I had no idea. No wonder I was such a wreck. And you were so patient with me. And you found the donkey! I can't wait to show you the photos. I just got them this week. Please come."

Marlee couldn't think of a way to ask if Matteo would be there, so she just accepted the invitation and decided to act as if he would be there even though she knew it was a one-in-a-million chance.

She bought the most gorgeous dress she had ever owned. It was red, in keeping with the holiday spirit, but other than that, there was nothing Christmassy about it.

It was predawn mist, made into fabric. The neckline was daring, and the length was bold. She bought amazing heels to go with it.

She curled her hair and put on makeup. As she looked at herself in the mirror, Marlee was so aware of who she was.

Strong and confident.

And very, very beautiful.

Fiona and Mike were hosting the party at their new condo. It was already packed when Marlee arrived, and it took nearly half an hour to sort through all the people and figure out Matteo was not among them.

Still, all that mingling in search of him had brought her in contact with a lot of people.

After her initial disappointment that Matteo wasn't there, she relaxed. She was shocked by how much men liked her. She was shocked by how good she was at flirting!

And dancing. The lessons had helped her confidence, but she also carried something within herself from that wild street party and the fairy-tale wedding on Coconut Cay. She didn't feel in any way inhibited.

She relished the attention. It egged her on. And she found it so easy to let go, have fun.

"Here she is," Fiona called. "Marlee. Look who I've got on Boom-Boom."

What the heck was Boom-Boom?

Marlee did a whirling turn in the crush of people on the dance floor to find Fiona with her phone pointed at her.

She realized there was something on the screen of the phone. And then she went stock-still as she realized.

Boom-Boom was that new video app.

Matteo.

"Marlee," he said.

He was thousands of miles away. He was talking to her through a screen. His voice felt as if it touched her.

"Matteo."

She was shocked by how he looked. His hair was too long. He looked gaunt. There was something haunted in his eyes when he looked at her.

And hungry.

And yet his tone was cool. "It's good to see you," he said. "I'm sorry. I seem to have a bad—"

And then the picture died.

And so did all the fun she had been having.

CHAPTER NINETEEN

MATTEO STARED AT the blank screen of his phone. Breaking that connection had been the hardest thing he had ever done.

Marlee had been so beautiful. So radiant.

As Fiona moved through the crowds with her phone, he had spotted Marlee well before she knew he was watching. He had seen her dancing. If it was possible, she had come even more into herself than she had on the cay.

Marlee's movements were totally sensual, made even more so by her confidence and her comfort with herself.

Matteo had seen the look on the man's face that she was dancing with.

He was enraptured with her.

And then she had turned, and there had been that moment's hesitation before she knew it was him.

Sometimes a man came face-to-face with his own weakness.

Because the look on her face made him want to beg, just as he had known he would have if he had stayed on Coconut Cay the night of the wedding.

She had been shocked to see him, and then the shock had melted to a pure welcome, which had made him feel weak.

Be with me.

He was changed since he had come back from Coconut Cay, and not in a good way. Marlee, it seemed obvious, had changed in good ways. She radiated confidence.

He, on the other hand, did not miss the fact his sisters were exchanging worried glances behind his back.

But here was the terrifying truth: if three days with Marlee had made him feel this empty, this bereft for a life without her in it, what would following these feelings do?

Because if he was to give in to the temptation to see what a life with Marlee held, one day, no matter how hard they tried to hold it off, they would say goodbye to each other.

And if he had known her a lifetime, instead of a few days, he would be like his father. It would not be survivable.

And what if he went first? What if he went first and left her to live in a world they had made bright together, and now there was nothing but darkness remaining?

Not, Matteo reminded himself, that Marlee had looked like she was suffering in the world without him in it. Not in the way he was suffering in the world without her.

Still, he'd done the right thing. To shut off the phone. To not feed his hunger to drink her in, to look at her, to let that unexpected glimpse of her feed his spirit.

He was aware he was not as strong as he wanted to be.

Because he went to his computer. He went to the photos that Fiona had just sent him. And he knew another sleepless night lay ahead of him as he drank his fill of the wedding pictures.

The bride and groom interested him only slightly.

It was her, Marlee, that he went to, again and again. One picture in particular made him look at it endlessly, trying unsuccessfully to grasp some secret it held.

"But we haven't looked at the photos yet," Fiona protested when Marlee announced, as soon as she could do so without being too obvious the call with Matteo had upset her, that she had to go.

"Let's do it another time," Marlee said with fake brightness. "There's so much going on here tonight. We have a bit of catching up to do. We haven't had a chance to talk about the baby, even."

"Let me see you to the door."

They stepped outside the noise of the party. Rain pattered on the porch roof.

"Thanks for going to see my mom," Fiona said. "I love that about you. You really care about people."

She *did* really care about people, and the look on Matteo's face was making her feel distressed.

"Did you notice?" Fiona said. "She's sober. And so excited about being a grandmother. She wasn't even mad at me about having a wedding she couldn't come to because she's scared to fly. She said she knew I did it on purpose. That it was the wake-up call that she needed."

"I'm glad for you. Things tend to work out, don't they?"

Did they? She wished she believed that just a little more strongly. After seeing Matteo, she suddenly wasn't that sure.

"I have something for you." Fiona handed Marlee a gift.

It was wrapped but obviously one of the wedding photos. Marlee decided to wait until she got home to open it.

"You look so gorgeous," Fiona said. "I've always known you had that hiding in you."

Not that your choice of dress had been a clue, Marlee thought dryly.

They hugged and promised to get together again soon. And then Marlee went home to her troubled thoughts.

Sitting alone in her living room, she opened Fiona's gift.

She had expected a framed picture of the bride and groom. But instead, it was a picture of herself and Henri. She was nose to nose with the adorable troublemaker, bestowing a kiss.

She radiated light.

A woman in love. And not with a donkey, either.

And Matteo, slightly out of focus, was in the background. But even out of focus, there was a particular look on his face as he watched her.

It was so clear he was a man who cherished her.

The truth was evident in the gaze that rested on her—possessive, protective, utterly entranced.

It was not a look that said—in any way—that she wasn't good enough. And it wasn't a look that suggested that their worlds were stratospheres apart, separated by chasms that could not be crossed.

Matteo looked so beautiful in this picture. As light-filled as she herself looked. Confident. *Sure*.

And yet, tonight he had looked so *awful*.

There was no other way to describe the brief

glimpse she had caught of his face before the connection died. She went to bed thinking about it, distressed by it, trying to decipher it.

It could be anything. A bad day on the markets. A poor business decision. Expensive problems with the jet! There were a thousand things that could have been troubling Matteo, and she had no hope of guessing what it was.

But when Marlee woke suddenly, in the middle of the night, she *knew*.

She knew what was troubling Matteo. The look on his face had been the look of a man who had touched a dream he knew he would not ever allow himself to have.

And Marlee was pretty sure that dream was her.

And that every single thing she had done since she got back to Seattle—her embracing of life— had been in preparation for the biggest challenge of all. It was as if she had been in training.

She had to be more confident of herself than she had ever been.

She had to know her strength.

She had to be braver than she had ever been.

She had to rescue Matteo from the lonely life he had set himself up for. With her blankets wrapped around her against the damp chill in her apartment, she went and found her computer.

It occurred to her that the third barrier—her

own sense of inadequacy—had already been overcome.

That left only the physical barrier of distance.

It seemed paltry in comparison. She looked up flights to Switzerland. The closer you got to Christmas, the less choice there was and the more expensive they became.

There was one on Monday.

Three days away.

She hadn't gotten that brave. She could not be that spontaneous. She could not just travel halfway around the world because she thought a photo had revealed a secret to her.

She told herself it was crazy. Worse than crazy. Absolute insanity.

She had never been to Zurich.

That's what map apps are for, an inner voice told her with shocking confidence.

She didn't have a clue where he lived.

You know the name of his company, though.

He had an international lifestyle. She didn't even know if he would be there when she arrived.

Could there be anything better than chasing true love around the globe?

Stop it, Marlee told her inner voice. *We have to be practical.*

Fiona and Mike's wedding had already nearly emptied her meager savings account.

Plus, she couldn't just not show up for work. She wasn't that kind of person. People counted on her to be dependable.

And the days before Christmas were so busy at the library. In fact, on Monday they were having a special guest—a wildlife refuge was going to bring a real live reindeer to story time. How could she not be there to supervise that?

But not one rational thought could stop her.

When the button popped up saying "Purchase seat", she pointed her mouse at it, lined it up, took a deep breath and clicked.

It felt, for all the world, as if she was a warrior who had just let loose an arrow.

She snapped the computer shut and waited for the fear and doubt to set in. She went back to bed. She lay there with her eyes open.

She hoped she could get her money back.

But when morning came, Marlee was shocked to find she was no more interested in getting her money back, no more willing to back down, than she had been when she had clicked on that purchase button.

She didn't really lose her nerve until she was in the back of a cab in a foreign country. In her other life, a reindeer would be entering the library right about now!

Everything she saw reminded Marlee she

was not in her own world. The cab driver had greeted her in three languages before settling on English. There was snow on the ground, which was rare in rainy Seattle. To her American eyes, Zurich had a fairy-tale-like atmosphere, with its old castle-like structures, cobbled roads, twisting streets.

She was dropped off in front of a very old building. There was a beautifully carved sign hanging over the street on a wrought iron arm—Monte Rosa Alpen.

So she was in the right place. There was a storefront and offices above it. She went to the display window and looked in.

There was an array of outdoor items: cross-country skis, snowshoes, what might have been a survival stove of some sort.

But what caught her eye was a beautiful, belted, woven jacket.

Oddly, that was what gave her courage. She wasn't a stranger here. She knew about this company. She knew about the great-great-great-grandmother who had started it.

What a courageous woman that long-ago Rosa must have been, striking out in a man's world.

As she opened the door, Marlee felt as if she might be channeling some of that long-ago courage.

The entry to the store was on her left and a narrow staircase went up to the right. She followed it and came to a glass door with the company name emblazoned on it.

What was she going to say?

No doubt some snooty secretary would send her on her way. Matteo probably worked in an impenetrable fortress. He was rich. He was powerful. Even if you had traversed the globe to do it, seeing him wasn't as easy as just waltzing into his office. Was it?

Taking a deep breath, she opened the door and stepped in.

The office space was soothing. The old bricks were exposed, and there was deep, inviting, leather furniture. There was a striking photo on the wall of the sun rising over a mountain, and Marlee assumed it must be Monte Rosa.

There was a counter and a woman behind it.

She looked up, startled, obviously not expecting anyone so early.

"Yes?" she called.

Marlee found herself frozen. She didn't know what to say. She debated turning and running. Her heart was beating so hard.

He could be anywhere, but Marlee could *feel* it. Matteo was here. Somewhere. Possibly, just feet from her.

The woman's face softened. "You're her," she said softly.

"Wh-who?" Marlee managed to stammer.

"The woman in the photo. I'm Emma."

"His sister. What photo?"

"You know who I am," Emma said approvingly. "He's spoken to you about his family. Go. Second door on the right. Don't knock."

Marlee went down the hallway. She felt as if she was in a dream, floating. She opened the door and stepped inside it. She closed it behind her.

Matteo was behind a desk.

He glanced up.

There were shadows in his face that had not been there before. His hair was too long, and he had not shaved.

Beloved, she thought.

His expression was stunned, and in that moment, Marlee saw everything she needed to see. She saw the reason she had come.

His expression quickly shut down.

"This is a surprise," he said, as if it wasn't a good one.

"Isn't it?"

She came toward the desk, paused in front of it, and then changed course. She scooted behind it. He got up from his chair, backing away from her. He shoved a framed photo face-down first.

"What are you doing here?"

She picked up the photo. She smiled. It was the same one Fiona had given her.

"This really is a good picture," she said.

"It's okay."

"Why do you have it on your desk?"

He was silent.

"Is it because you love me madly?" she asked him softly.

"Don't be ridiculous. We barely know each other."

"Barely," she said. "That reminds me of swimming in your pool."

He actually blushed. He looked flustered.

"Why do you have a picture of someone you *barely* know on your desk, Matteo?"

"I like the composition," he said. "The donkey."

"Uh-huh." That could be insulting, but she was not insulted. The truth felt as if it shimmered in the air between them.

"Do you miss me?" she asked softly.

Silence.

"Do memories of being in each other's arms keep you awake at night?"

Silence.

"Do you dream of my lips on your eyes and your ears, on your chest and your—"

"Stop it!" he said, his voice a croak. "This is all so wrong."

CHAPTER TWENTY

"Wrong?" Marlee asked Matteo, stunned.

"It's not what you deserve. An affair? You? The world's most decent girl?"

"I was trying out being an outlaw," she reminded him.

"Well, it was a poor fit. It became more than evident that you are not that kind of woman."

"I've realized that. In fact, it seems almost funny that once upon a time I believed a cigar and a sip of rum could change something fundamental about me."

He nodded. "You're decent to the core," he said. "It's obvious."

"Was it when we were swimming in your pool that it became that obvious to you?" Marlee goaded him a bit.

"That was no more who you are than the rum and the cigar."

She smiled. "I disagree. You see, smoking and drinking are just outside things. They could never change what's inside a person. But that day in the pool—"

He interrupted her, obviously not wanting to think about the skinny-dip in his pool!

"I knew," he said firmly, stubbornly, "as soon as I saw Fiona in her wedding dress how wrong it all was. That's what you deserve. Underneath it all, you're an old-fashioned girl. You deserve forever. Commitment. I thought you had realized it, too. I thought that's why you did your Cinderella exit from the reception."

"No. Some old insecurities reared their ugly heads. They said I was making a fool of myself over you."

Matteo looked stricken. "You weren't," he said, making an effort to wipe the distressed look off his face. "In fact, you looked as if you'd embraced that part of yourself quite nicely when I saw you at Mike and Fiona's Christmas party."

"I think I have embraced lots of parts of myself quite nicely. That's what I'm trying to tell you, Matteo. When I got home, I realized it wasn't about changing myself with silly things like cigars and rum. It wasn't really about changing myself at all. It was about uncovering who I really was, inside, not outside. You gave me the courage to take that journey. To learn how to live."

He was silent.

"Can we talk about forever?" Marlee asked softly. "Since you brought it up?"

"Yes," he said harshly. "Let's talk about it. There's no such thing. Look at the marriage statistics. Abysmal."

He grabbed his phone out of his pocket, tapped away furiously. "Fifty percent end in separation or divorce." He held up the screen so she could see the cold, hard evidence. It felt as if he was holding up a shield.

"That means fifty percent don't," Marlee pointed out mildly. "My parents have been happily married for thirty years. That's my model for being married."

"You're thinking about being married?" he said. "Who said anything about being married?"

"Uh, I think you might have mentioned it."

"Not in the context of *us*," he said. "Like you and me. Married."

"I wasn't suggesting tomorrow. I thought we could have a courtship first. You know, nice and old-fashioned. Exactly what you've decided I deserve."

He was silent. But she thought she saw a faint flicker of hope in his eyes.

"Your parents would have been married forever, too," she said softly. "If your mom had made it."

"Well, she didn't!" he said.

And just like that, they were at the heart of the issue.

"Those few days with you, Matteo, gave me courage I've never had before to embrace life completely. To really live. To find out who I really was, and then to be that. That was your gift to me."

Still, he was silent.

"Do you know why I'm here?"

He shook his head, mute.

"To return that gift to you. To give you the courage to embrace life completely, to really live. To ask you to take the biggest risk of all. To risk loving me, even though there might be pain involved."

"The pain might be yours," he warned her.

Which, he seemed to realize, was not an out-and-out no. He glared at her.

"It might be," she agreed. "You'd like to protect me from that, wouldn't you?"

"I saw what happened to my father."

"Yes, you did. You're not just trying to protect yourself, are you? You're trying to protect me?"

After a long time, he nodded, accepting that he had been unmasked.

"If we can feel this strongly after such a short time," he said, his voice with rough edges to it, "what would it be like to lose each other? After a year? After ten years? After a lifetime?"

"We can't look at all the things that could happen. It would make it impossible to live life, let alone fall in love."

"It's part of what I do," he said stubbornly. "I'm a businessman. I do the cost-benefit analysis. I ferret out all the things that could go wrong."

"And where does choice figure into your calculations, my darling?"

He could have flinched at the use of the endearment. Instead, she watched as he softened toward her.

"Your father made a choice, Matteo, to let his pain break him instead of make him stronger. He made a choice not to see he had three beautiful children carrying the legacy of his and your mother's love into the future."

He was leaning toward her as she crossed what remained of the small distance between them.

She laid her forehead against his forehead and took both his hands in her own. The sensation of his skin against her skin was like a homecoming.

"I think," she said, ever so softly, "a bigger risk than not loving someone because they might die is dying a slow, painful death inside each and every day because you have not loved someone. Be brave, Matteo. We can write our own ending. Say yes."

His voice was a whisper, but it was enough.

"Yes."

She took his lips with her own, with welcome and hunger. At first, he answered, but then he pulled away.

"No," he said. "If we're going to have a happy ending, I must prove to myself I can be a better man—"

"I like the man you are now just fine," she assured him.

But he shook his head, vehement. "I can be everything you deserve. I want to treat you with complete respect and honor."

"I never felt disrespected or dishonored," she said.

"If I can't keep my hands off you, it clouds everything."

"But in the best possible way."

"No," he said. "It's going to be an old-fashioned courtship, worthy of you, or nothing at all."

"If those are your terms, I accept," she said and held out her hand.

When he took it, she pulled him to her and kissed him soundly on the mouth.

Finally, he pulled away from her. "You don't intend to make this easy, do you?"

"Absolutely not," she warned him. And then she took his lips again.

And he answered, and they explored peaks higher than Monte Rosa. Finally, he broke away.

Flustered, he glared at her.

"If you can keep your lips off me for a few minutes—"

"Nearly impossible, but I'll try."

"I can make a plan. For our courtship. How long can you stay?"

"If I combine my Christmas holidays with a few days of annual leave, I could stay until just after the New Year. But don't make a plan. Let's just be spontaneous."

"That's not a good idea," he decided. "That's what got us into trouble in the first place."

"Outlaws like me love a little trouble," she told him.

"Behave yourself. I'm going to introduce you to my sister."

That night, after being thoroughly wooed over the best dinner she had ever eaten, Marlee was dropped off by Matteo at the hotel room he'd insisted on booking.

His good-night kiss was disappointingly gentlemanly, despite her efforts to tempt him. Now, alone, which was also disappointing, she took in her accommodations.

The room was like a room in a palace. And

she felt as if the prince had found her slipper after all.

And there was something quite adorable about him having to try so hard to keep his hands off her!

She called home.

"Um, Mom, I'm in Switzerland."

"What? Where? Have you lost your mind?"

"Maybe. I don't think I'm going to be home for Christmas."

"Not home for Christmas?" In her family this was akin to saying you would be playing a tambourine in an airport with a money collection basket at your feet.

"Mom, I've met someone."

"In Switzerland," her mother said, flatly.

"No, I met him at Fiona's wedding."

"The man from the picture!" her mother said, her whole tone changing entirely.

"What? What picture?"

"Fiona has some posted online on Chatter or whatever that app is called."

"You have the Chatter app?" Marlee asked, astounded.

"You're not the only one full of surprises," her mother said dryly, and then added, with relief in her voice, "That's totally different. You know him. He's friends with Fiona and Mike.

You know what your father said when he saw the picture of you and that man and the donkey?"

"No, what did he say?"

"He said, there's the man who is going to marry our daughter."

Was her mother crying? "He did not," Marlee said.

"Do you want to ask him? James, it's Marlee. She's in Switzerland with that man from the picture."

"The news is on. Tell her hello."

That was more like it! Chatty Cathy, indeed.

"He never did like Arthur," her mother confided.

"Did you?"

Her mother hesitated. "I just wanted whatever would make you happy."

In the next few days, it felt as if Marlee discovered an even deeper well of happiness than she had found on Coconut Cay.

Because if there was one thing better than Switzerland at Christmastime, it was being in in Switzerland at Christmastime and being madly in love.

Matteo wanted to show her *everything.* They explored the Christmas markets in Zurich's old town and admired the fifty-foot Christmas tree at the train station. They went to Château de

Chillon and Rhine Falls, and they took a dinner cruise on Lake Zurich.

They spent Christmas with his family and Marlee loved his sisters and his brothers-in-law and his two nieces and his two nephews instantly.

And they loved her.

"We've been waiting for you," Mia told her as they did dishes together after Christmas dinner. "I've never seen him so happy. You could not have given us a better gift."

One of the best parts of it all was the wonderful game they were playing, where he tried to resist the temptations she offered him—he still clung to the ridiculous notion that he must now be a perfect gentleman—and she played outlaw to his gentleman by trying to seduce him.

She was winning, and she found it so endearing that he felt guilty about that, as if by finding her totally irresistible he was failing her in some way!

The ten days went by in the blink of an eye.

But then, just as she thought the ball was over, and they were going to have to navigate the lonely days of a long-distance relationship, Matteo granted reprieve.

The day before she was supposed to fly home on the commercial flight she had booked, he informed her he'd cleared his schedule.

"I'm going to fly you home," he said.

She widened her eyes at him. "Does this mean we're going to join the mile-high club?"

She loved it when she did this to him. He was shocked. He sputtered.

"I'm going to meet your family. Have mercy, Marlee."

But she didn't.

Once they arrived, he insisted on staying in a hotel, and even though Marlee felt like that particular horse had already fled the barn, she could tell her father approved mightily of the arrangement.

His approval just made Matteo even more convinced that their courtship should remain unclouded by passion.

And made her more determined to test him at every turn.

It made the most delicious of tensions build between them as they explored her hometown together.

She kissed him madly at the top of the Space Needle, and again in the middle of the crowded Pike Place Market. She didn't work at the Central Library, but she took him to it anyway, because it was the flagship of the Seattle Public Library system and an architectural wonder. It felt particularly naughty dragging him behind the bookcases for an extended kiss!

They spent time at her apartment, but only

if she promised to keep her hands off him. So they did ordinary things. Who knew that baking cookies and playing Scrabble and watching movies could make anticipation build to a place that was so painful you just had to give in to it?

It rained and it rained and it rained.

And her life had never felt so light-filled.

The day came when he had to leave. But the light did not go out. In fact, impossibly, beautifully, their relationship intensified.

He sent flowers.

She sent love notes.

They video-chatted deep into the night. He read her poems. She read him a funny story. They used an app that allowed them to watch movies together.

He sent his jet and they spent a wonderful weekend in Venice. After they'd been apart, his resolve was absurdly easy to overcome. They never even got to ride a gondola! The next time he sent the jet, they went to Paris. She was sure the Eiffel Tower and the Louvre couldn't compare to drinking hot chocolate in bed, anyway.

Saying yes instead of no was really an affirmation that the whole universe seemed to turn its ear to, Matteo had discovered.

Of course, he was saying yes to some activities he had promised himself he would say no to, but no man was perfect, after all. There were temptations no one could be expected to resist, and Marlee made sure he knew that.

He did penance for his weakness by pulling out all the stops in his courtship of Marlee. He made sure every single thing about them falling more and more in love was worthy of the fairy-tale ending.

Now, Matteo had never been so nervous in his life. Marlee didn't even know he was back in Seattle. In what he considered a proper culmination to their romance, he was meeting Marlee's father for lunch. He wished he could be meeting him with a clearer conscience.

And if the meeting with her father went well, he already had a ring, purchased from the best jeweler in Switzerland.

"Mr. Copeland—"

"What? Jimmy."

"Uh...okay, Jim. As you might have noticed, Marlee and I have been spending quite a bit of time together. It's become quite serious. I mean, I've been honorable. Tried to be honorable... What should I order?" he asked, panicking and switching tack.

Mr. Copeland—Jimmy—was looking at him, clearly baffled. "We're in Seattle," he said, as if Matteo needed reminding, and maybe he did. "Seafood is always a good bet."

Matteo stared at the menu. Seafood. Where was he? Speaking of "fish," he wanted to fish in his pocket and have a quick glance at his talking points.

Treated her with honor.

Wooed her.

Old-fashioned respect.

Well, for the most part.

"Spit it out, man," Marlee's father said, not unkindly.

"I love your daughter. I can't even think straight for it anymore. I want your permission to marry her."

Jim Copeland was smiling broadly at him. "It's about time, son. Of course you have my permission. But who asks the dad's permission in this day and age, anyway?"

Matteo could tell he was pleased despite his protest.

And this old-fashioned request felt as if it confirmed what he had been working toward all this time: to be worthy of being not just Marlee's lover—for where was the worth in that?—but worthy of being her husband.

It was pouring rain—did it do anything else here?—an hour later when Matteo knocked on her apartment door.

The look on her face when she opened it said it all.

Surprise became delight.

Delight melted into heat.

She threw herself into his arms.

And he could not wait one minute longer. He slipped the box from his pocket and held it out to her.

"A cigar box?" she asked, puzzled.

"Open it."

She did. Still puzzled, she reached for the cigar. And then she saw what encircled it. The ring flashed bright against the brown paper of the cigar.

"Yes!" she squealed.

"I haven't asked you yet. Stop it. I'm getting down on one knee and—"

"You stop it! Yes, you have asked me. You've asked me a million different ways on a hundred different days."

"Marlee!"

"Okay, okay," she said. She was quivering with excitement.

He sank to one knee and gazed up at her.

"I love you madly," he said. "I cannot picture a life without you in it. You have made me a better man. Braver than I ever imagined I could be. Wide-open to the adventure of life in a way I never was before. I want you to marry me. I want you to be my wife. I want to walk all the rest of my days with you at my side. I cannot imagine a life without you in it."

She reached for his hand. She drew him to his feet. She handed him back the cigar, and he took the ring from it and slid it onto her finger.

She didn't even glance at it. She really didn't care if it was a million-dollar ring from the best jeweler in Switzerland, or if it was a dime-store ring from the corner confectionery by her apartment.

"Yes," she whispered.

The cigar fell to the floor between them.

EPILOGUE

MATTEO SAT ON the beach alone, his arms wrapped around his knees, his feet dug deep into the sand. He was waiting for the sun to come up, and it was one of the rarest of moments on Coconut Cay. Except for the gentle lap of the waves, it was absolutely quiet.

The beach was not yet transformed. In a few hours, the arbor would be going up, the gardenias woven through it. A piano would be brought down, along with a registry table. There would be chairs—one hundred and fifty of them, at last count—set up on the sand, facing the arbor and the sea.

Matteo sighed.

This was *not* what he and Marlee had planned.

No, they had planned to celebrate their meeting on Coconut Cay with a quiet exchange of vows. They had wanted to ride donkeys down to the private pink sand beach Mackay had shown them over a year ago. They had wanted to say "I do" as a tropical sun set and gilded the entire island in gold.

Then, they had thought they would have one

reception in Zurich for his family and friends, and one in Seattle for hers.

The problems had really started when his sisters had caught wind of the plan.

They had been appalled.

Because they thought his and Marlee's wedding plans separated them into two families.

"We're one family now," Emma had informed him sternly.

Never mind the logistics of several thousand miles and an ocean between them. Never mind the logistics of figuring out which of the great-aunts and old friends and second cousins and work colleagues could be asked to make this incredible journey.

Meanwhile, Fiona, high off the success of her own wedding, had started a wedding planning business. Before Matteo and Marlee quite knew what had happened, they were being swept up in Fiona's plans for them.

Fiona was not even slightly slowed down by that adorable baby she now had on her hip most of the time.

Matteo had never considered himself a "baby" guy. In the past, he had found the charm others found in the little creatures quite baffling. When his nieces and nephews had been babies, he had found them to be shockingly boneless little bundles filled with puke and poo. He would do the obligatory uncle-holds-the-baby-and-gets-rid-of-it-as-soon-as-possible.

But that little girl of Fiona's absolutely melted him. She had a smile Matteo was convinced she reserved only for him. He even held her sometimes and was always taken aback by the deep longing he felt when that baby nestled into him.

For the love he shared with Marlee to be made manifest in a child. A little girl or a little boy that he would call Calamity when he teased and chased him or her around wildflower-strewn meadows in the Alps.

Matteo would have thought Marlee would have wanted more say in her own wedding plans, but she laughed at the very suggestion.

"I planned a wedding once," she reminded him. "Devoted myself to it. Every little detail *mattered.* And yet somehow, I was missing what mattered most of all."

How grateful he was that that event had never happened, a reminder to both him and Marlee of silver linings in the clouds of life.

"Planning a wedding was nerve-racking," Marlee continued. "Not to mention time-consuming. Truly? I'm nothing but relieved to have someone else looking after all those endless and pesky details. It leaves me more time to, well, you know."

He did know.

She grinned that wicked outlaw grin that she reserved just for him.

And so now, really, their wedding was completely out of control. The budget was shot, the guest list was bloated, the whole island was bursting at the seams, and the logistics of bringing everything together in just a few hours was mind-blowing.

His wedding, Matteo mused, had a bit of a three-ring-circus feel to it.

Tomorrow, post-wedding, Fiona's mother, once so terrified of flying she had taken a miss on her daughter's own wedding, was going to celebrate one year of sobriety by organizing a skydiving excursion involving a frighteningly decrepit Coconut Cay airplane.

Naturally, the bride, not being the least sensitive of Matteo's fear of the death of the woman he had chosen to be his life partner, had been first to sign up!

Fiona had egged Marlee on, even suggesting she wear her dress. Ever since Fiona had been nominated for that bride photo of the year for that picture of her feeding her bouquet to Henri, she looked for photo opportunities everywhere.

It seemed to always be in the back of her mind as she organized flower girls and a ring bearer, caterers, florists, donkeys, musicians, special arrangements for Great-Aunt Hetta.

Matteo's wedding: the three-ring circus.

As he thought about it, the birds began to wake. They acted as if it was their job to sing the sun out of the sea, and the quiet air was soon split with a cacophony of sound as each bird tried to outdo the other in welcoming the new day.

Really, Matteo reflected, wasn't this exactly what he'd been missing since his mother died? Family was a three-ring circus: joyous, loud, colorful, a million different things unfolding at all times.

Then, a feather, pure and white—maybe a gift from one of those birds—drifted out of the sky and touched his cheek, feeling for all the world like the gentlest of kisses.

He took the feather and held it. For one stunning, beautiful moment, Matteo knew his mother was with him, and had always been with him, guiding him to this day.

To saying yes to love.

To realizing it was the one thing worth risking everything for.

He knew, of course, that he and Marlee were not promised a life without challenges. Hardships. Losses.

Just as he knew this was the message from his mother: that it was the power of love that sustained the human spirit, even through unfathomable sorrow.

In the face of it all, love was the only real power.

That sense was confirmed a few hours later, as he was standing under the arbor. He was wearing a simple white linen shirt and dark slacks, and he was barefoot. Mike was at his side. Waiting.

They came first: family, his giggling nieces tossing flower petals, his nephews solemnly leading Henri and Calamity. The donkeys had bright pink hooves and each carried a ring on the matching pink pillow on their backs.

His nephews, Matteo noticed with enjoyment, had looks of pure terror on their faces, not from the donkeys or from the responsibility they'd been entrusted with, but undoubtedly from the fear of incurring Fiona's wrath if they blew this.

And here came Fiona, now in a hideous dress that she and Marlee had shrieked with laughter over as they chose it.

"My mother isn't the only one who knows how to make amends," Fiona had declared, admiring herself and twirling in the fluffy dress in the glorious shades of a three-day-old bruise.

And then, Matteo's whole world stopped as Marlee appeared.

Her mother was on one side of her and her father on the other, not so much giving their daughter to him as joining them all together in that ancient circle of love that was family.

He was only peripherally aware of her parents. All he could see was her.

Marlee.

She was not wearing a wedding gown. She had put her foot down with Fiona over that.

"In the heat?" she had said. "Forget it."

And he was so glad she had *forgotten* it. She came toward him in a white sheath that was exactly like her. Simple, unpretentious, natural. The dress sang of the summer that Marlee carried within her, even on the rainiest of days.

The most unnatural thing about her would be her toenails, which he had snuck into her room last night to painstakingly paint bright pink, to match Henri's and Calamity's. She had something Henri didn't have, though. There was an octopus on the fourth toe of each of her feet.

Marlee's smile put the sun to shame.

The look in her eyes as she gazed at him filled him to the top.

In Marlee's unfaltering stride, he could see everything that she had become, loving and being loved, unveiling her innate beauty layer by gorgeous layer.

And he could see his whole future walking toward him.

And it was brilliant.

* * * * *

*If you enjoyed this story,
check out these other great reads from
Cara Colter*

Snowbound with the Prince
The Wedding Planner's Christmas Wish
His Cinderella Next Door
Matchmaker and the Manhattan Millionaire

All available now!